HOUND HEROES

BEWARE THE CLAW!

By TODD GOLDMAN

TO MY ONE AND ONLY HERO:
MY DAUGHTER ELLE, WHO LIKE THE
HOUND HEROES, IS ALSO HOUSEBROKEN.

- TODD

Library of Congress Cataloging-in-Publication Data Available

ISBN: 978-1-338-64847-8 (hardcover)
ISBN: 978-1-338-64846-1 (paperback)

10 9 8 7 6 5 4 3 2 1   21 22 23 24 25

Printed in China   62

First edition, January 2021
Edited by Kristin Earhart and Michael Petranek
Lettering by Jessie Gang
Book design by Veronica Mang

THE HOUNDS

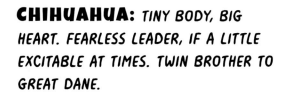

CHIHUAHUA: *TINY BODY, BIG HEART. FEARLESS LEADER, IF A LITTLE EXCITABLE AT TIMES. TWIN BROTHER TO GREAT DANE.*

GREAT DANE: *LOYAL AND KIND. EMOTIONAL AND A BIT OF A WORRYWART. TWIN BROTHER TO CHIHUAHUA.*

POODLE: *ACTIVE AND STRONG, SHE'D RATHER BE MUDDY AND MUCKY THAN PRIM AND PROPER.*

PUG: *THE BRAINS OF THE GANG. QUIET, BUT NOT SHY. SHE'S ALWAYS READY FOR ADVENTURE.*

SHEEPDOG: *LIGHTHEARTED, CAREFREE, AND ALWAYS READY TO PLAY PLAY PLAY!*

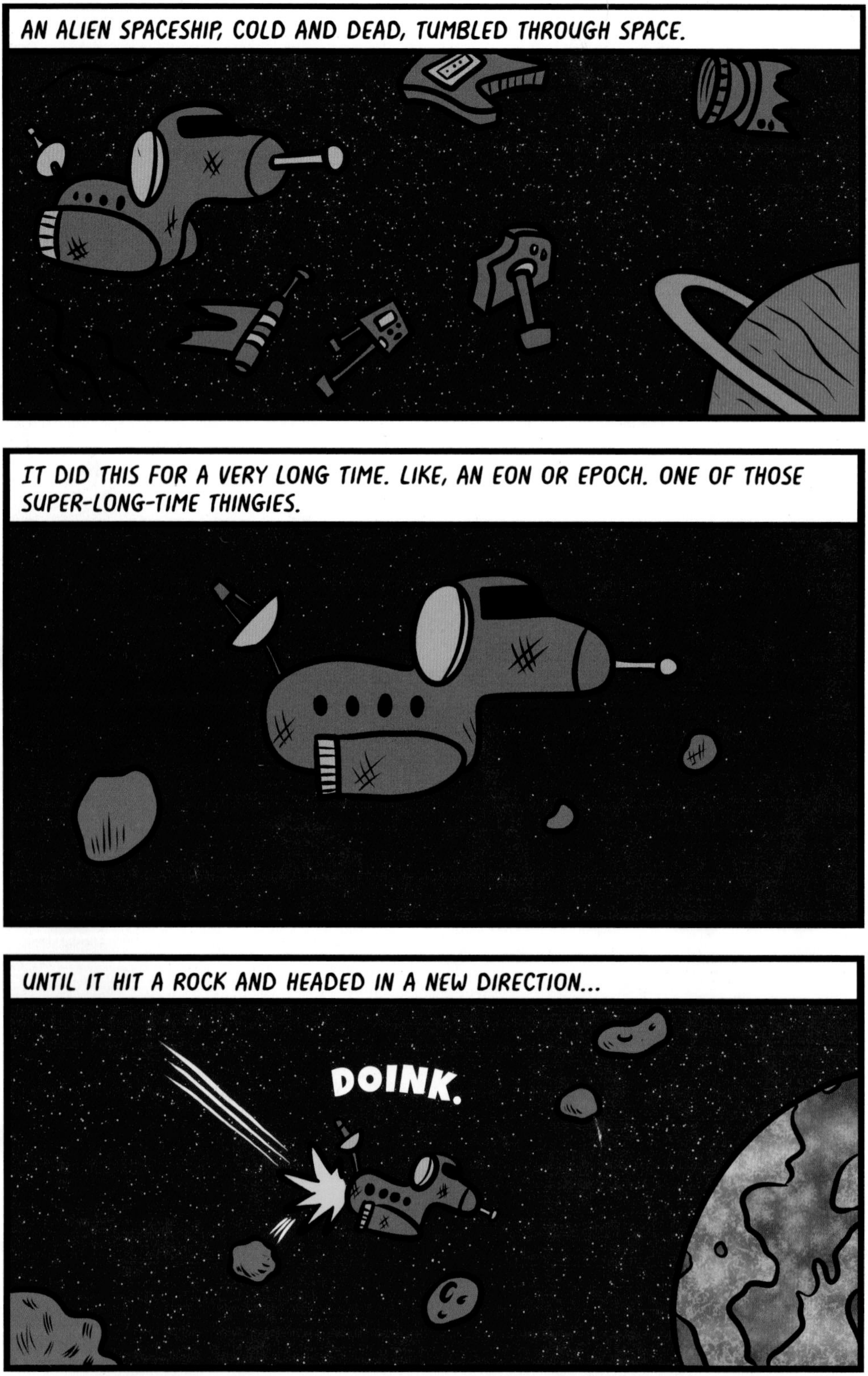
AN ALIEN SPACESHIP, COLD AND DEAD, TUMBLED THROUGH SPACE.
IT DID THIS FOR A VERY LONG TIME. LIKE, AN EON OR EPOCH. ONE OF THOSE SUPER-LONG-TIME THINGIES.
UNTIL IT HIT A ROCK AND HEADED IN A NEW DIRECTION...
DOINK.

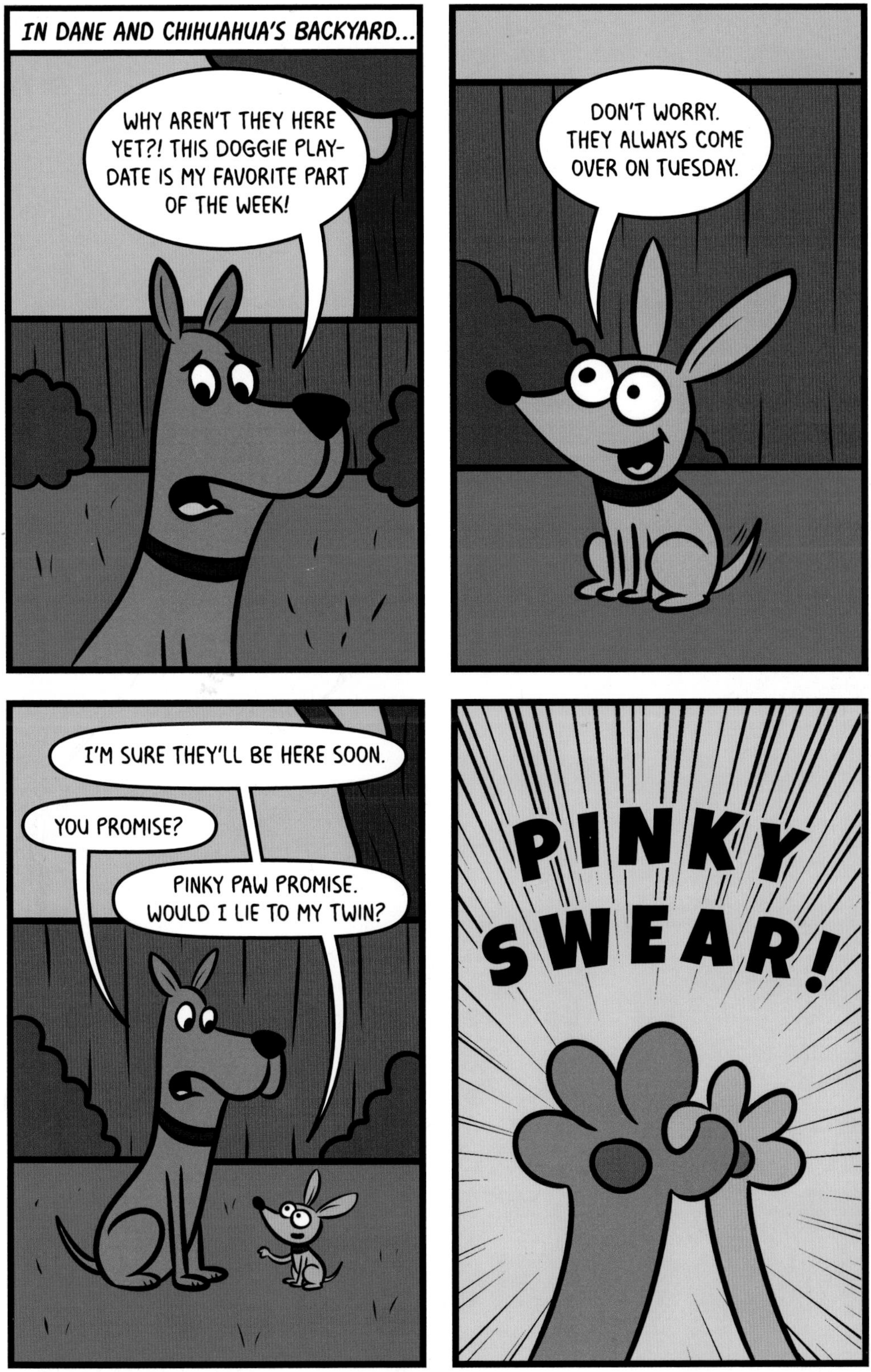
IN DANE AND CHIHUAHUA'S BACKYARD...
WHY AREN'T THEY HERE YET?! THIS DOGGIE PLAY-DATE IS MY FAVORITE PART OF THE WEEK!
DON'T WORRY. THEY ALWAYS COME OVER ON TUESDAY.
I'M SURE THEY'LL BE HERE SOON.
YOU PROMISE?
PINKY PAW PROMISE. WOULD I LIE TO MY TWIN?
PINKY SWEAR!

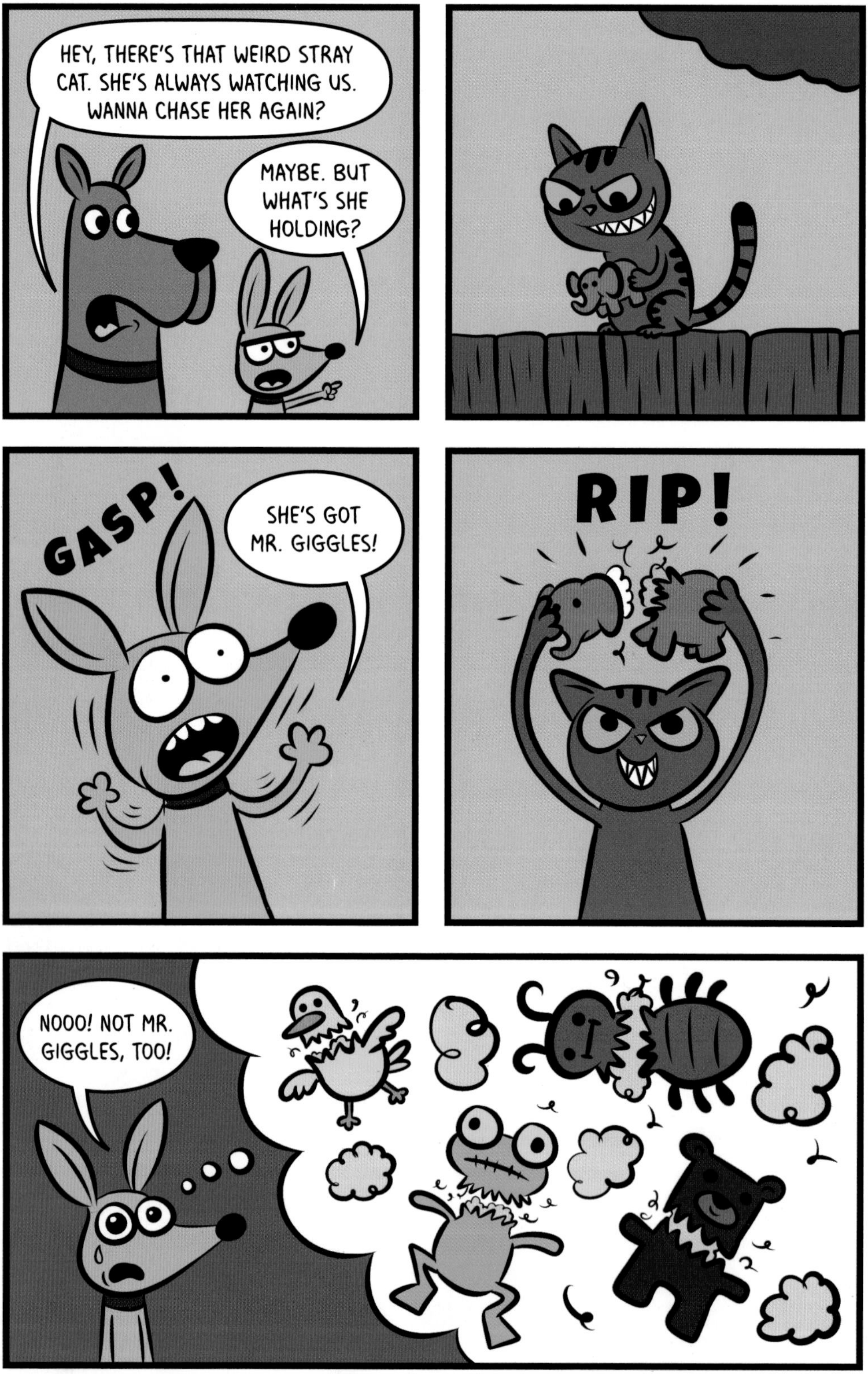
HEY, THERE'S THAT WEIRD STRAY CAT. SHE'S ALWAYS WATCHING US. WANNA CHASE HER AGAIN?
MAYBE. BUT WHAT'S SHE HOLDING?
GASP!
SHE'S GOT MR. GIGGLES!
RIP!
NOOO! NOT MR. GIGGLES, TOO!

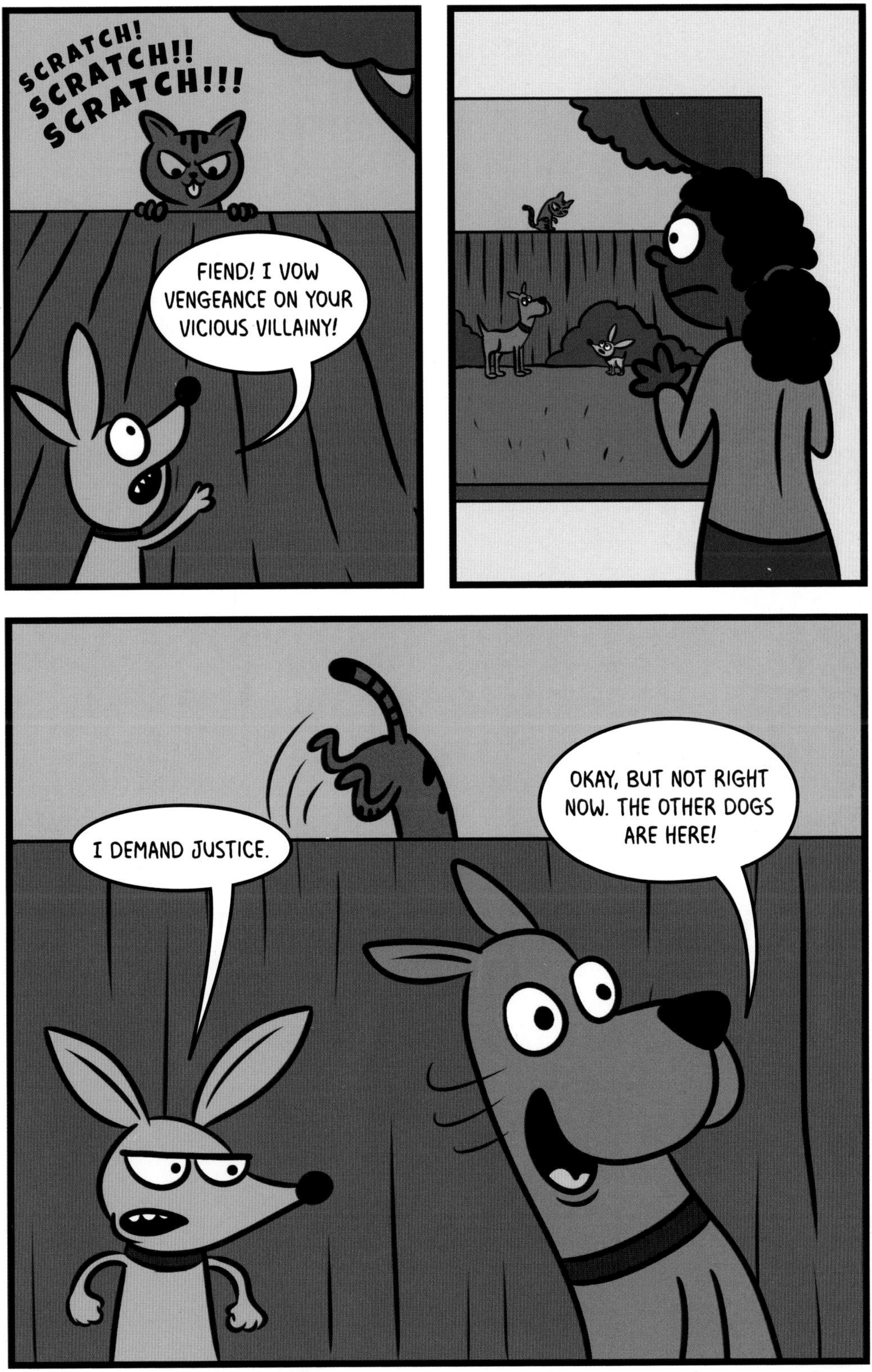
SCRATCH!
SCRATCH!!
SCRATCH!!!
FIEND! I VOW VENGEANCE ON YOUR VICIOUS VILLAINY!
I DEMAND JUSTICE.
OKAY, BUT NOT RIGHT NOW. THE OTHER DOGS ARE HERE!

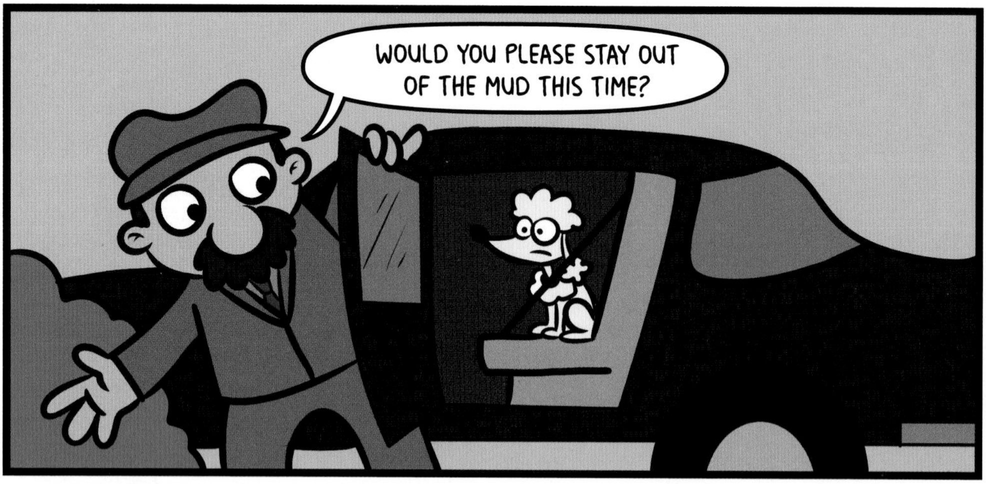
WOULD YOU PLEASE STAY OUT OF THE MUD THIS TIME?

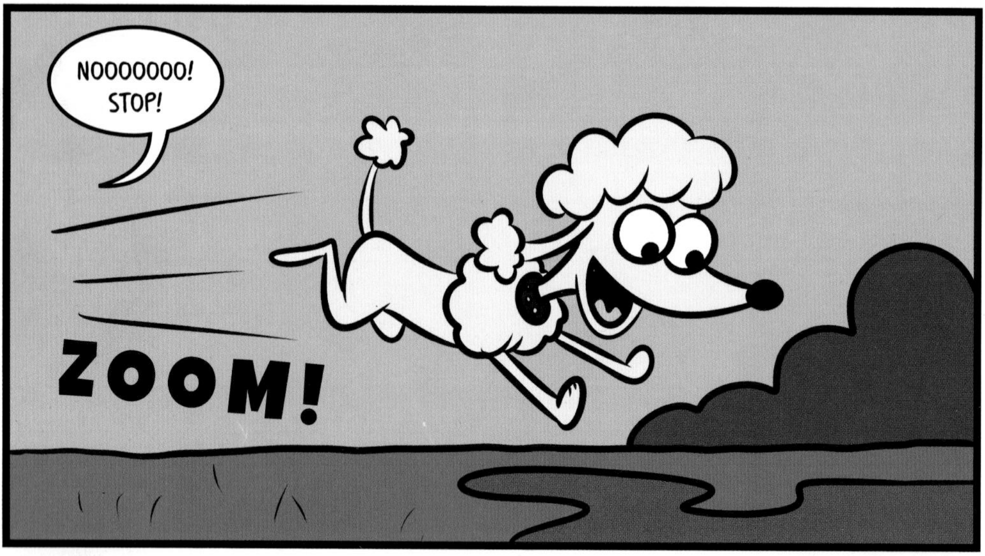
NOOOOOOO! STOP!
ZOOM!

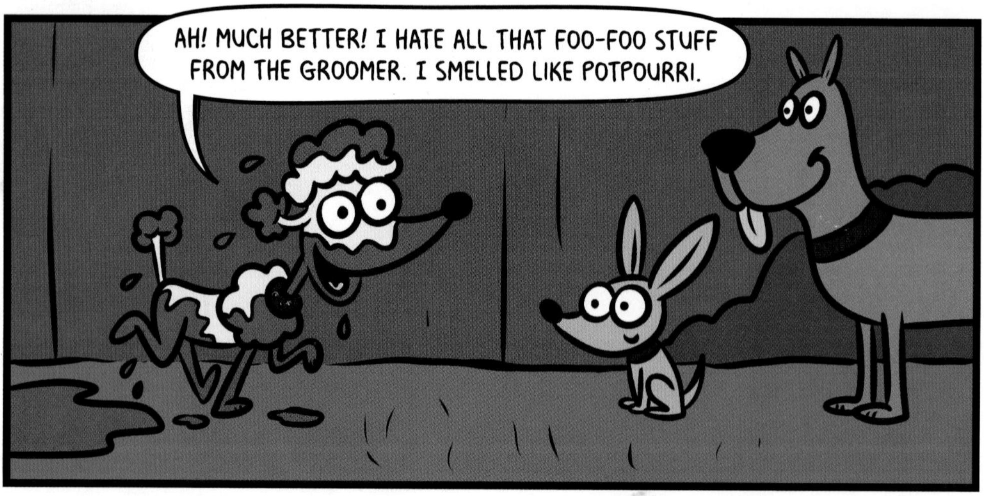
AH! MUCH BETTER! I HATE ALL THAT FOO-FOO STUFF FROM THE GROOMER. I SMELLED LIKE POTPOURRI.

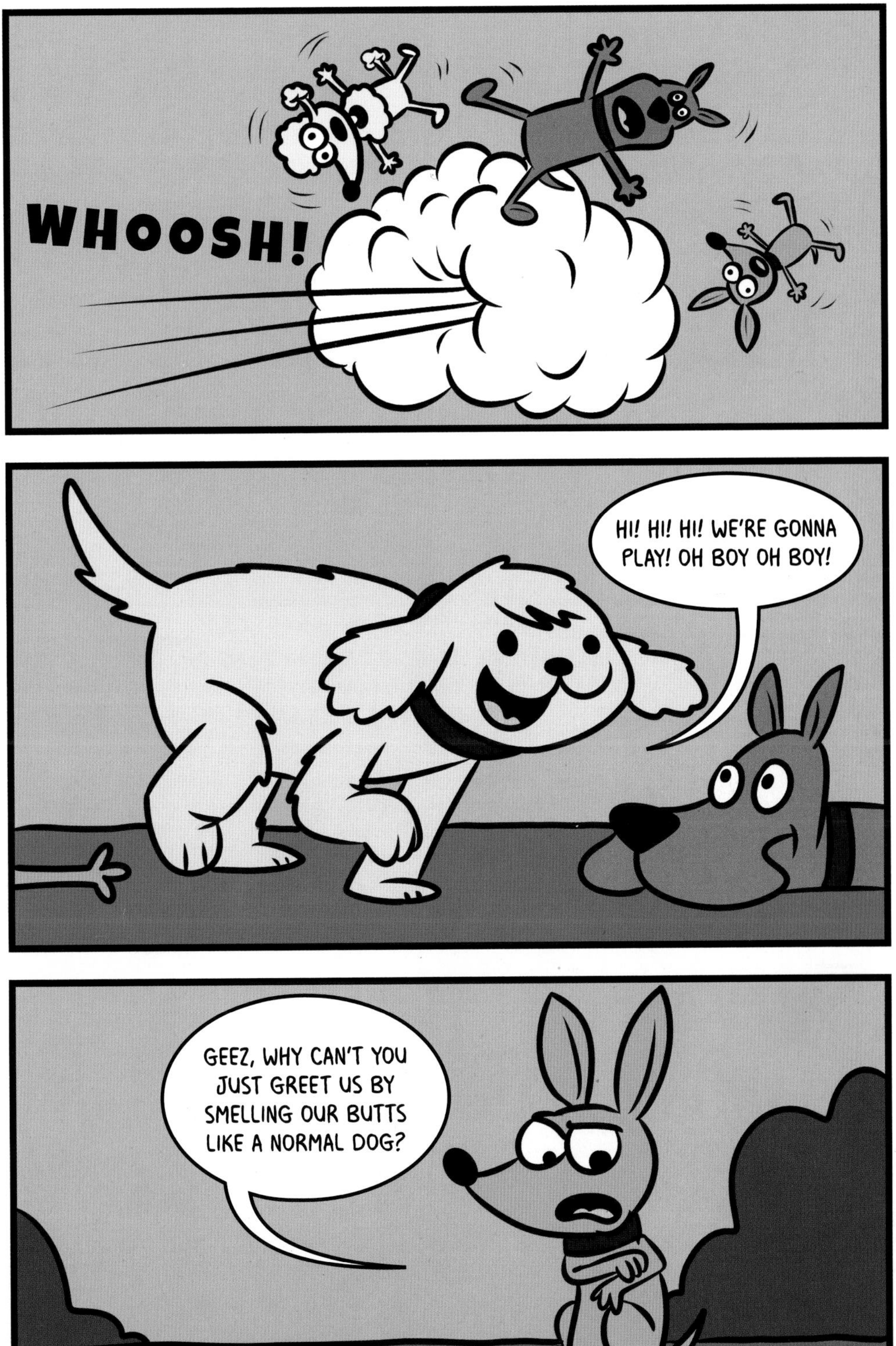
WHOOSH!
HI! HI! HI! WE'RE GONNA PLAY! OH BOY OH BOY!
GEEZ, WHY CAN'T YOU JUST GREET US BY SMELLING OUR BUTTS LIKE A NORMAL DOG?

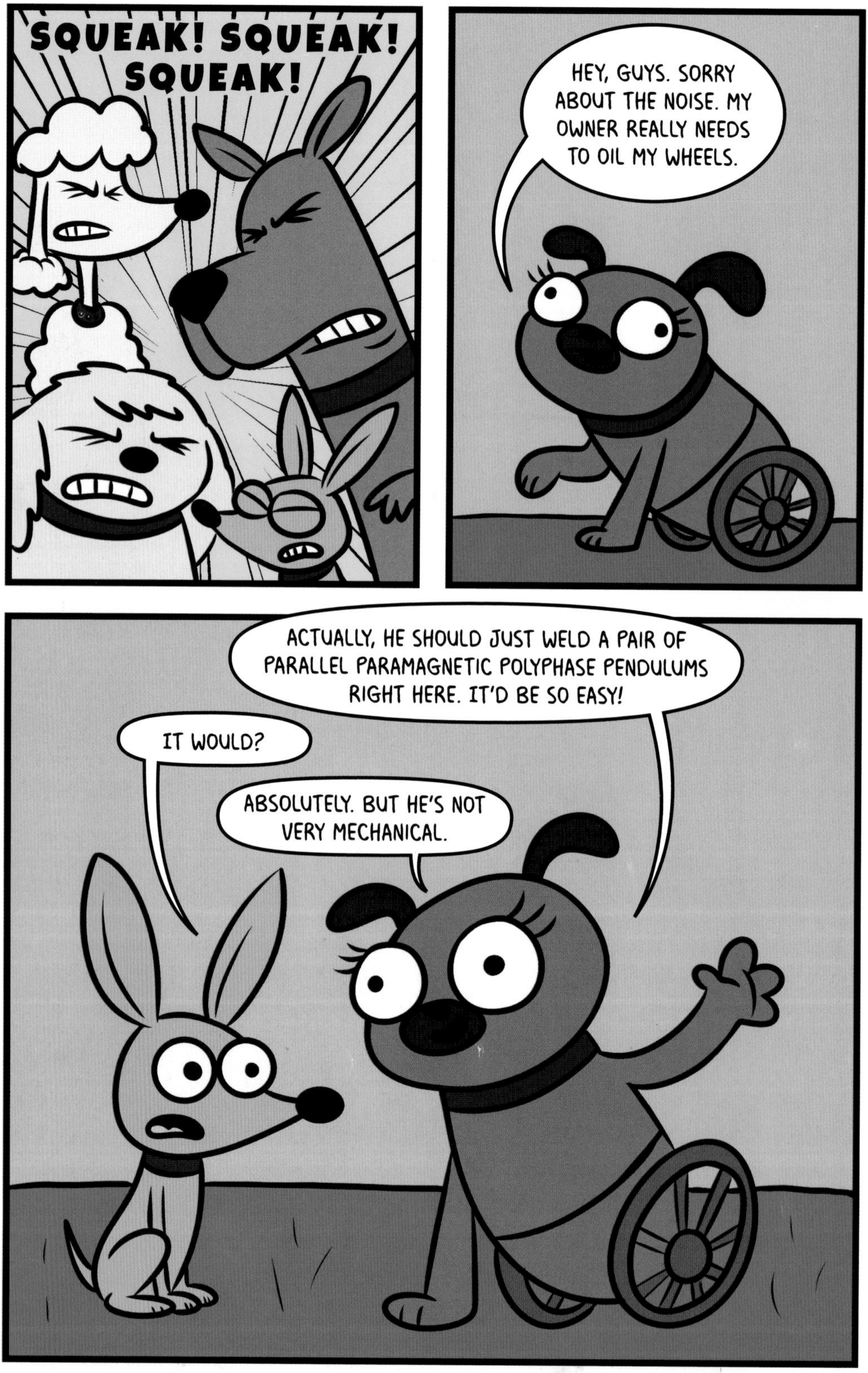
SQUEAK! SQUEAK! SQUEAK!
HEY, GUYS. SORRY ABOUT THE NOISE. MY OWNER REALLY NEEDS TO OIL MY WHEELS.
ACTUALLY, HE SHOULD JUST WELD A PAIR OF PARALLEL PARAMAGNETIC POLYPHASE PENDULUMS RIGHT HERE. IT'D BE SO EASY!
IT WOULD?
ABSOLUTELY. BUT HE'S NOT VERY MECHANICAL.

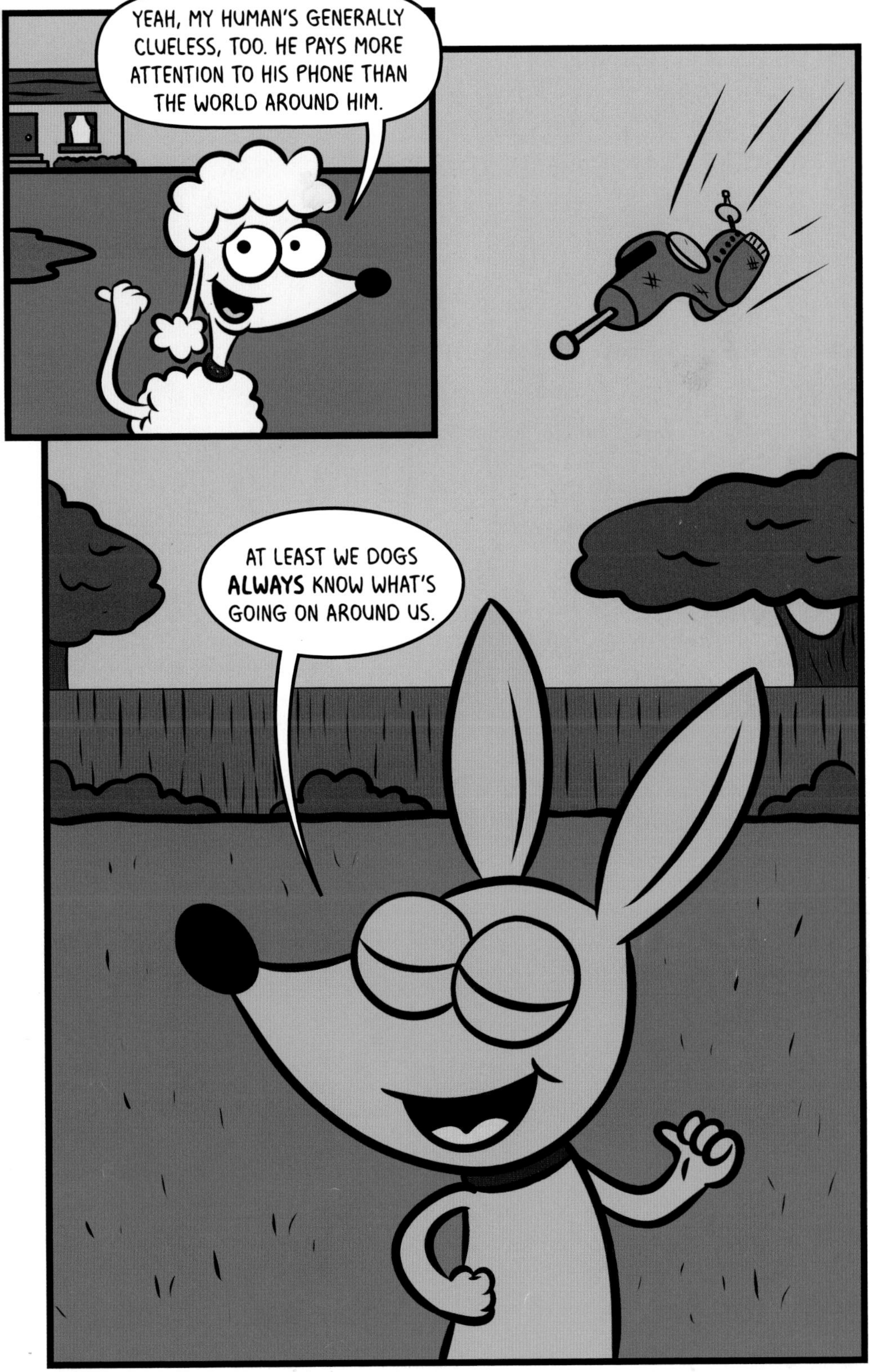
YEAH, MY HUMAN'S GENERALLY CLUELESS, TOO. HE PAYS MORE ATTENTION TO HIS PHONE THAN THE WORLD AROUND HIM.
AT LEAST WE DOGS **ALWAYS** KNOW WHAT'S GOING ON AROUND US.

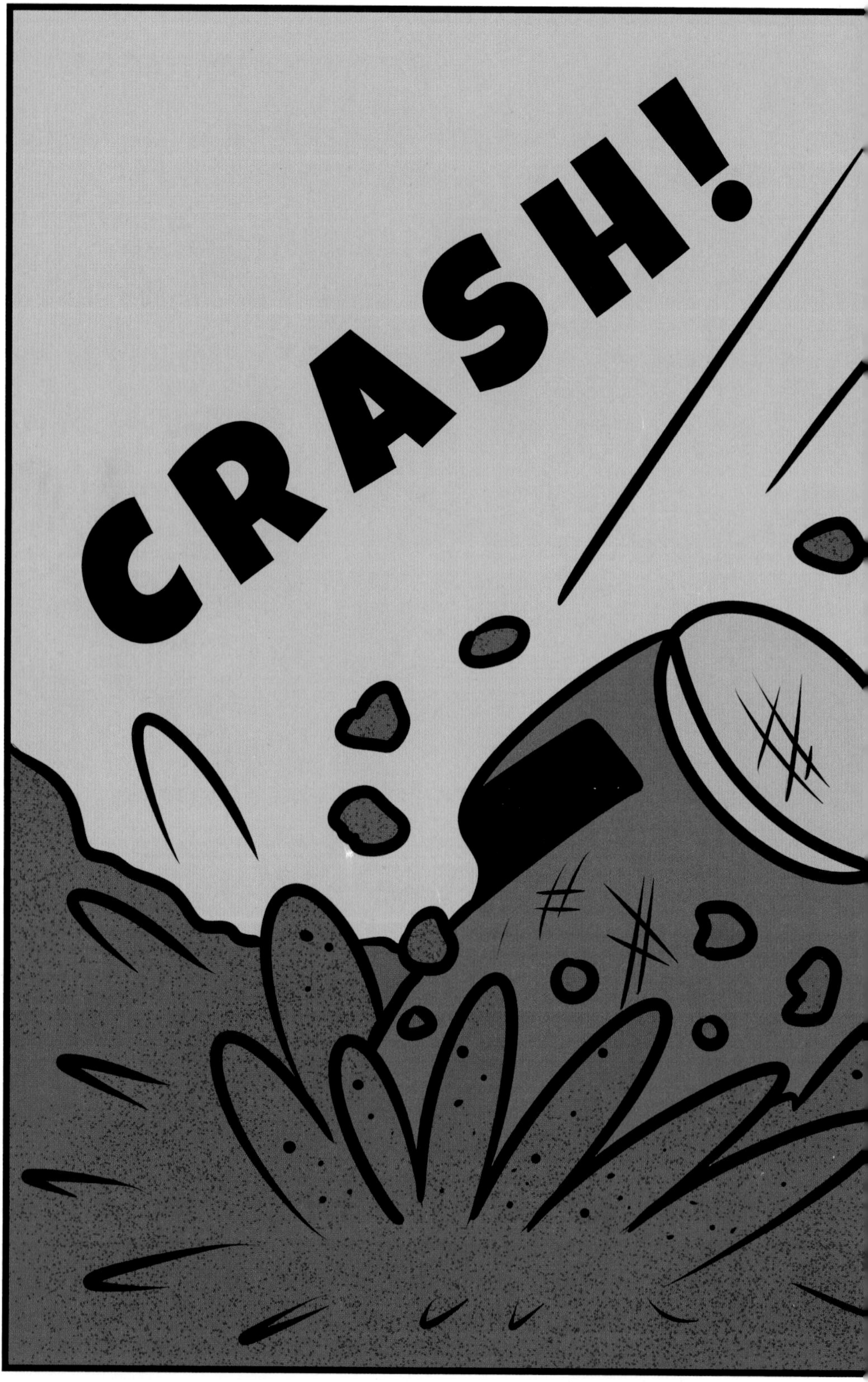
CRASH!

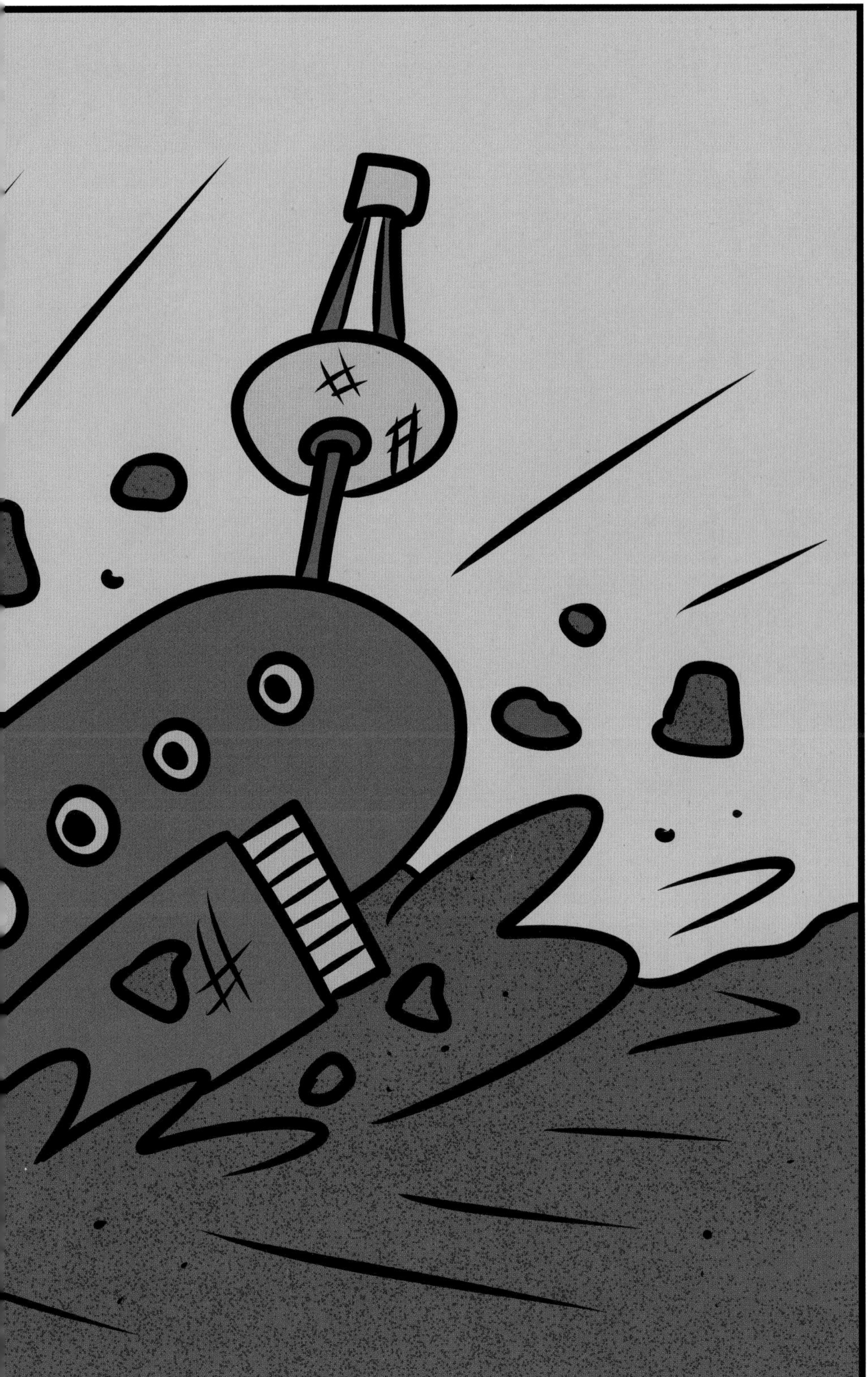

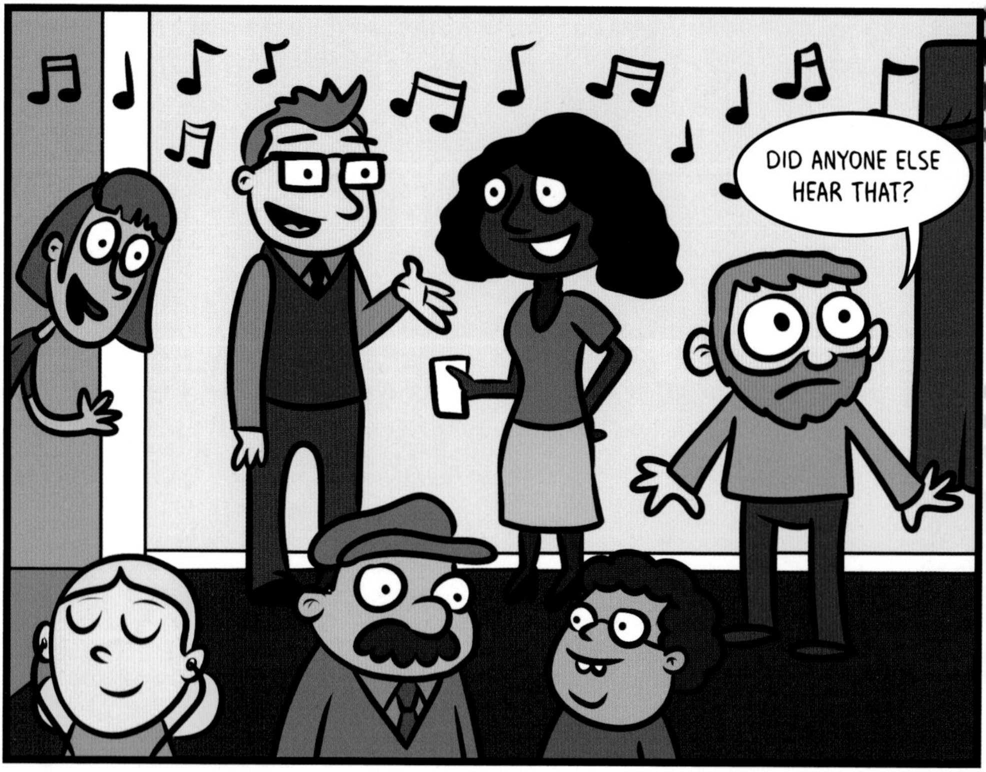
DID ANYONE ELSE HEAR THAT?

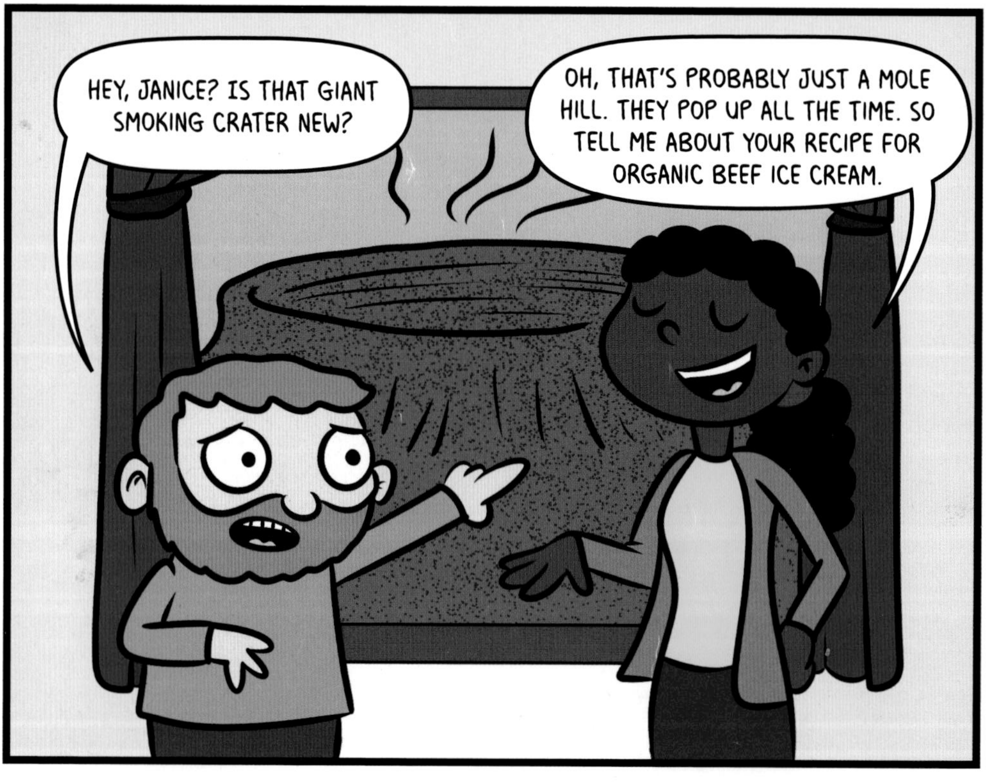
HEY, JANICE? IS THAT GIANT SMOKING CRATER NEW?
OH, THAT'S PROBABLY JUST A MOLE HILL. THEY POP UP ALL THE TIME. SO TELL ME ABOUT YOUR RECIPE FOR ORGANIC BEEF ICE CREAM.

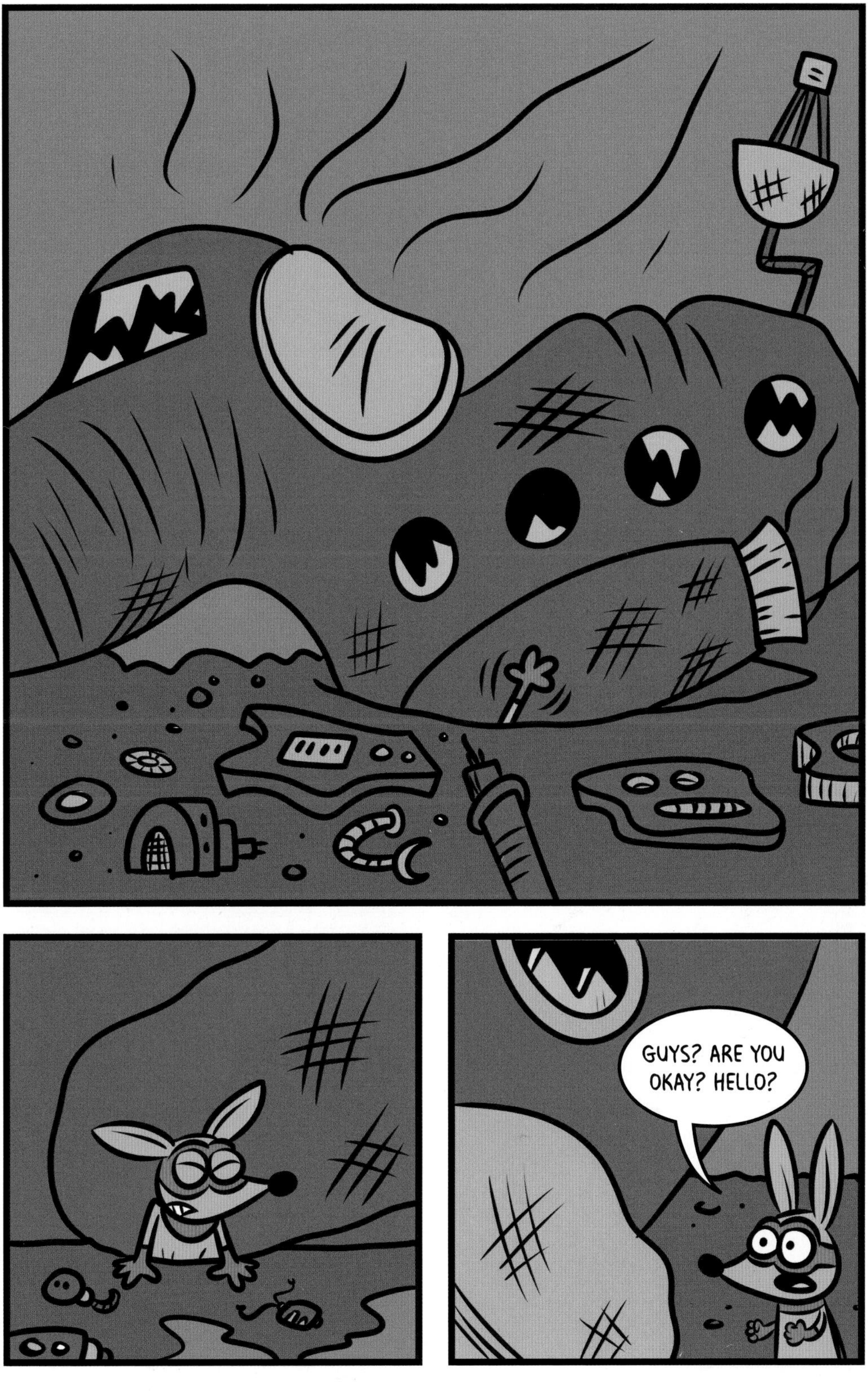
GUYS? ARE YOU OKAY? HELLO?

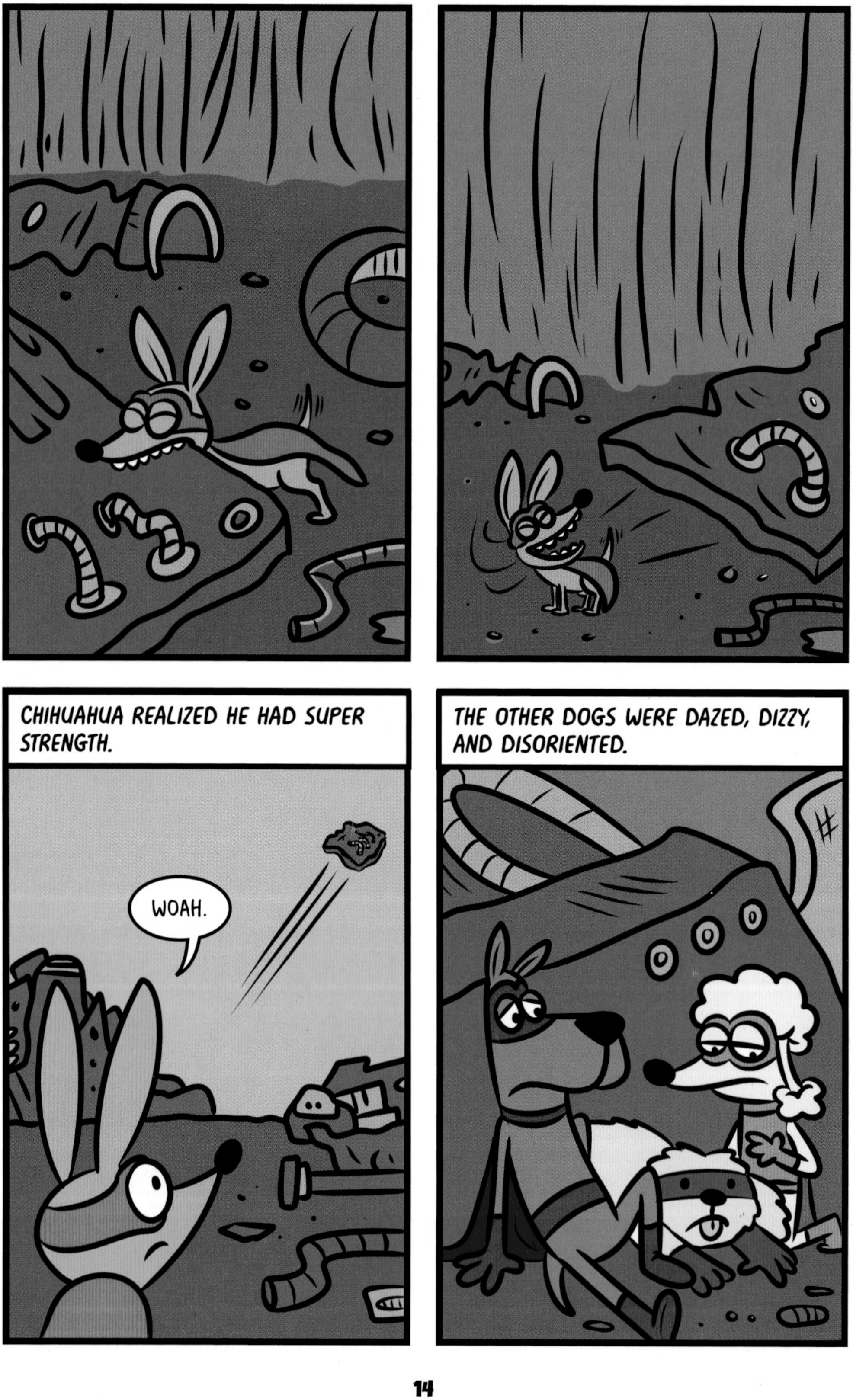
CHIHUAHUA REALIZED HE HAD SUPER STRENGTH.
WOAH.
THE OTHER DOGS WERE DAZED, DIZZY, AND DISORIENTED.

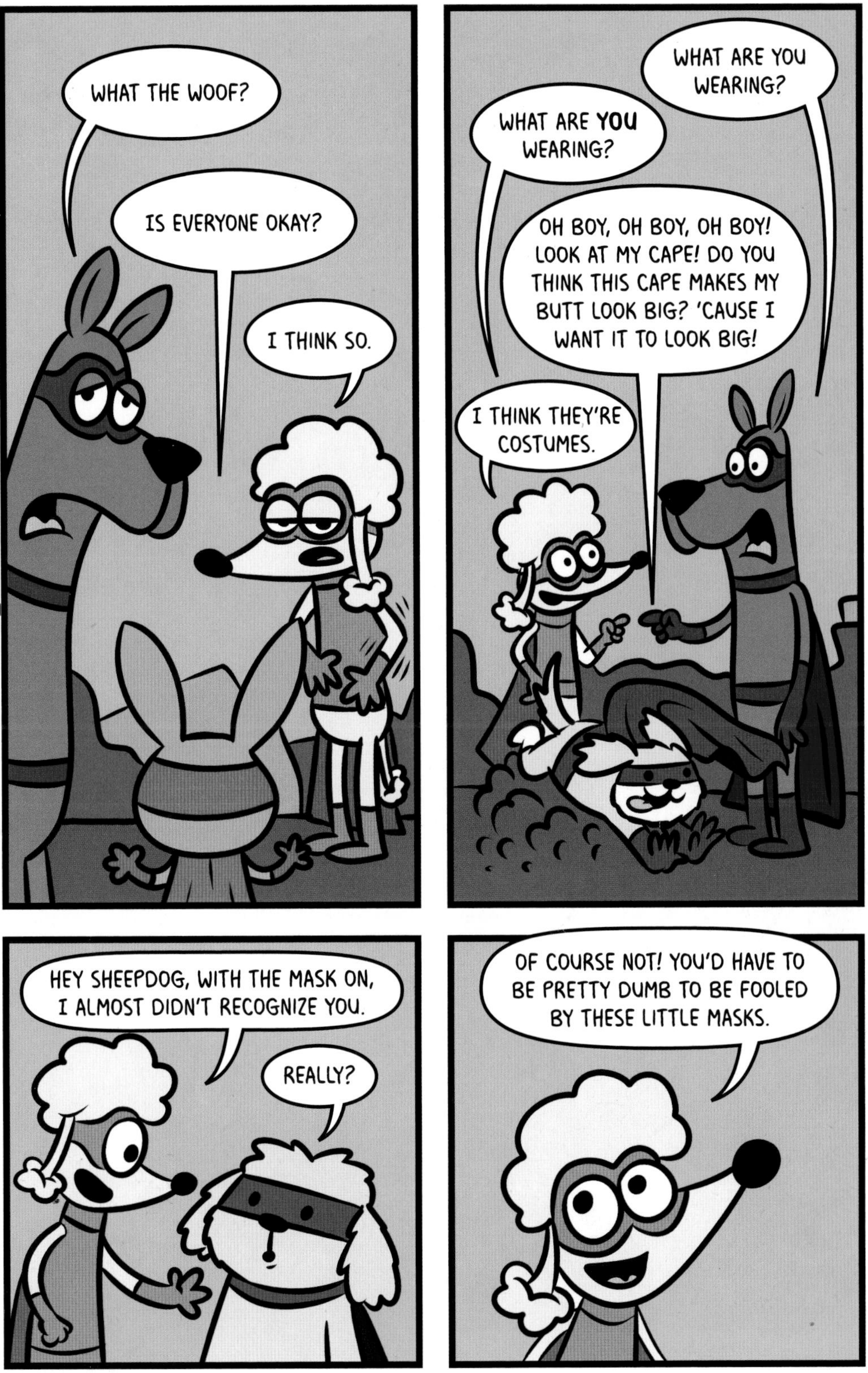
WHAT THE WOOF?
IS EVERYONE OKAY?
I THINK SO.
WHAT ARE YOU WEARING?
WHAT ARE **YOU** WEARING?
OH BOY, OH BOY, OH BOY! LOOK AT MY CAPE! DO YOU THINK THIS CAPE MAKES MY BUTT LOOK BIG? 'CAUSE I WANT IT TO LOOK BIG!
I THINK THEY'RE COSTUMES.
HEY SHEEPDOG, WITH THE MASK ON, I ALMOST DIDN'T RECOGNIZE YOU.
REALLY?
OF COURSE NOT! YOU'D HAVE TO BE PRETTY DUMB TO BE FOOLED BY THESE LITTLE MASKS.

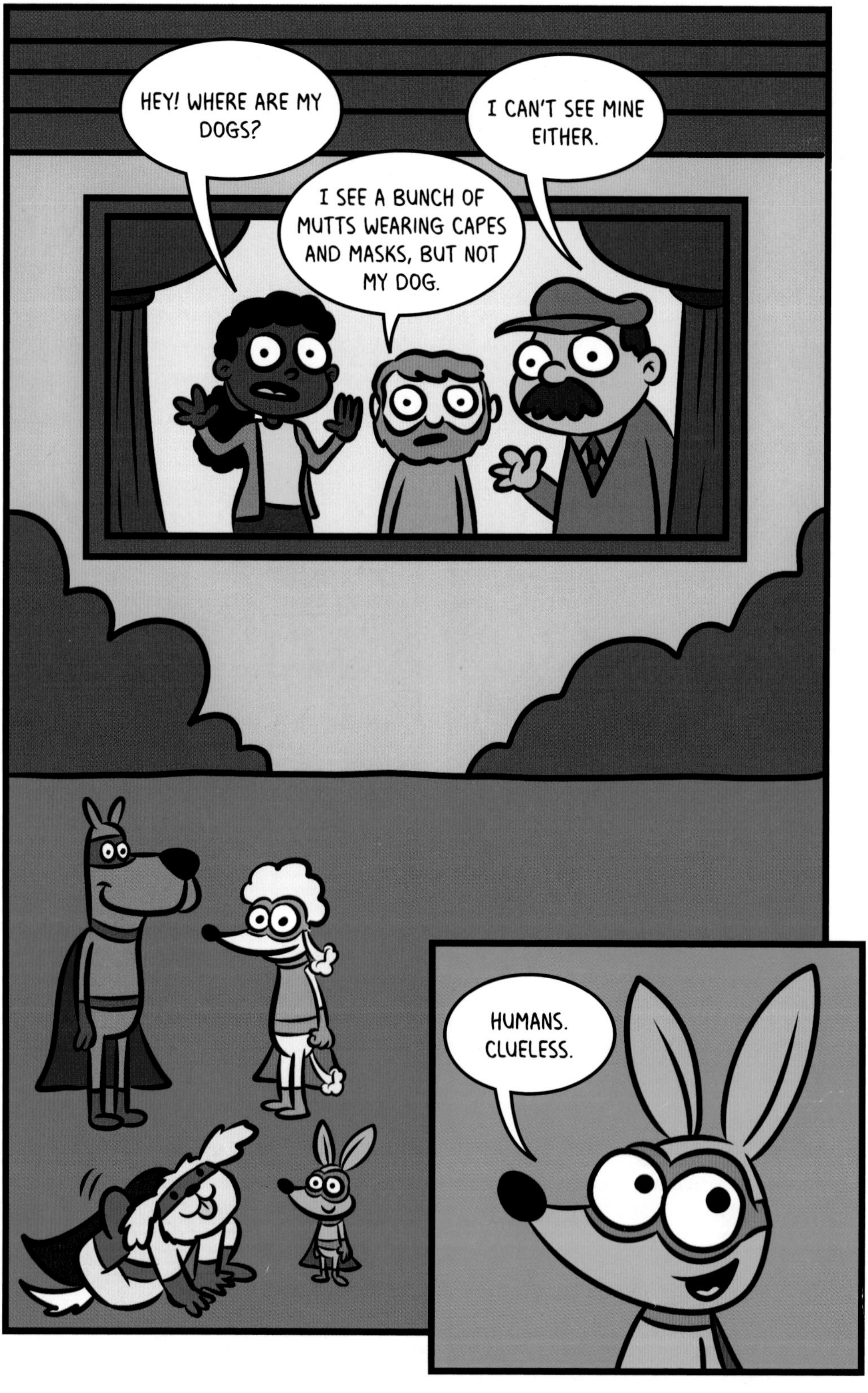
HEY! WHERE ARE MY DOGS?
I SEE A BUNCH OF MUTTS WEARING CAPES AND MASKS, BUT NOT MY DOG.
I CAN'T SEE MINE EITHER.
HUMANS. CLUELESS.

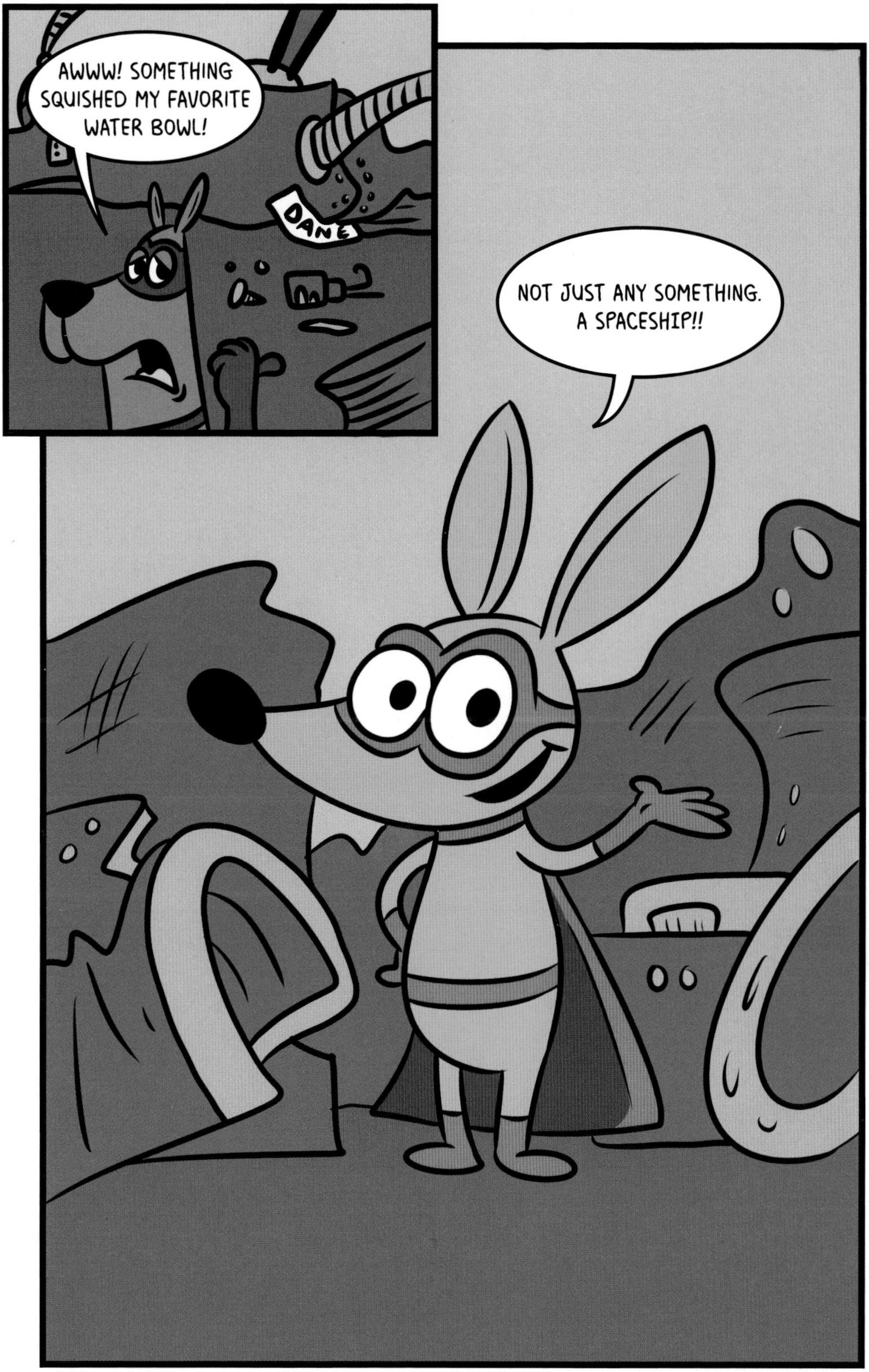
AWWW! SOMETHING SQUISHED MY FAVORITE WATER BOWL!
DANE
NOT JUST ANY SOMETHING. A SPACESHIP!!

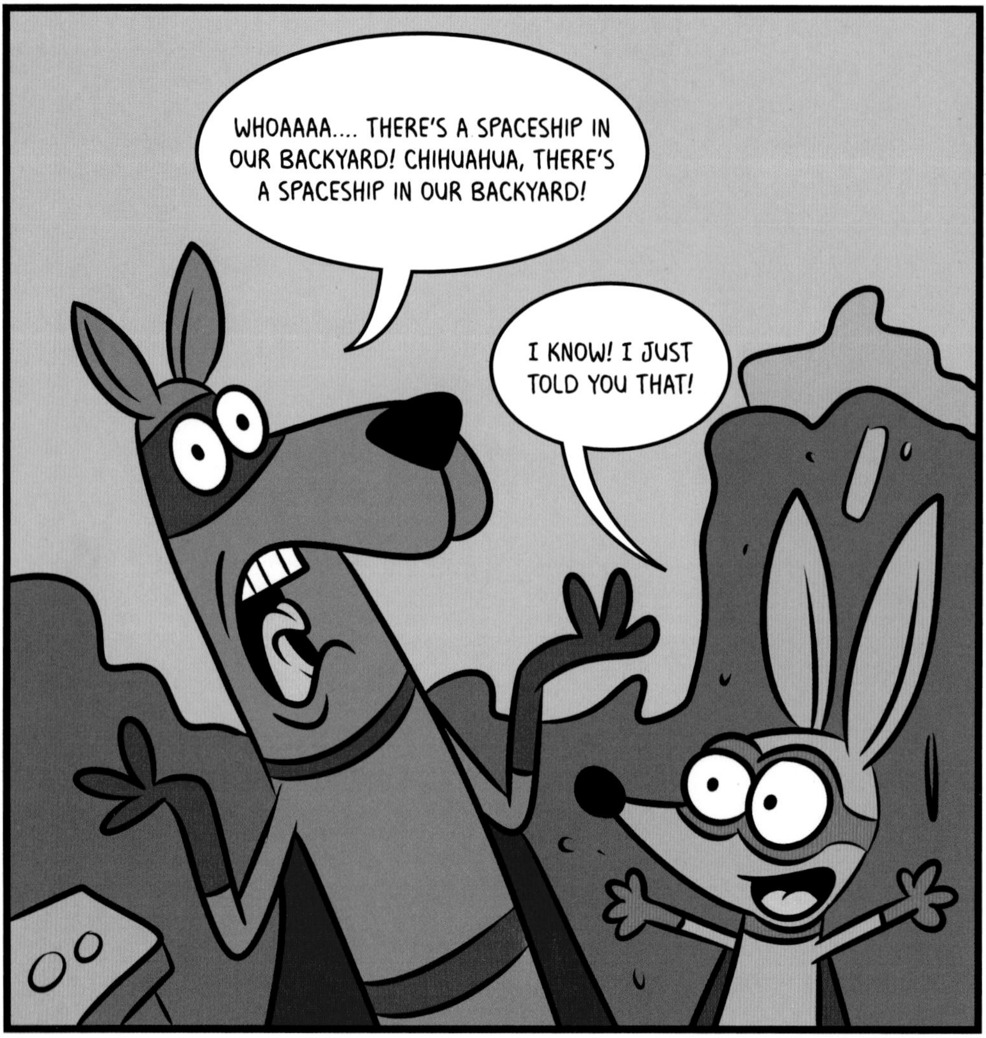
WHOAAAA.... THERE'S A SPACESHIP IN OUR BACKYARD! CHIHUAHUA, THERE'S A SPACESHIP IN OUR BACKYARD!
I KNOW! I JUST TOLD YOU THAT!

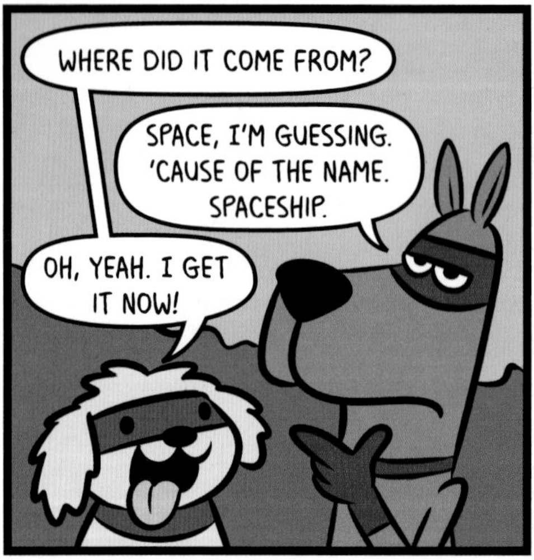
WHERE DID IT COME FROM?
SPACE, I'M GUESSING. 'CAUSE OF THE NAME. SPACESHIP.
OH, YEAH. I GET IT NOW!

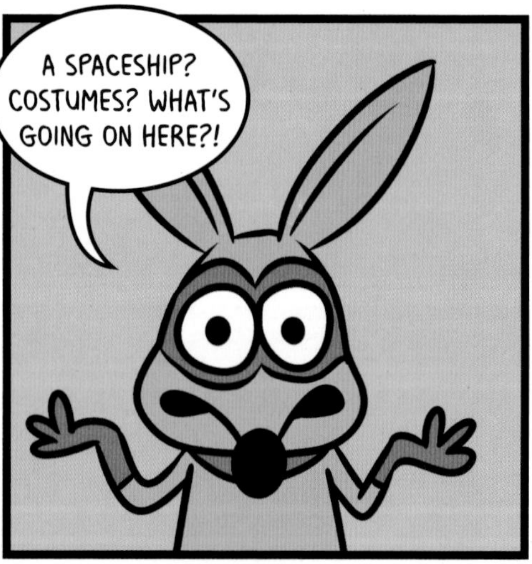
A SPACESHIP? COSTUMES? WHAT'S GOING ON HERE?!

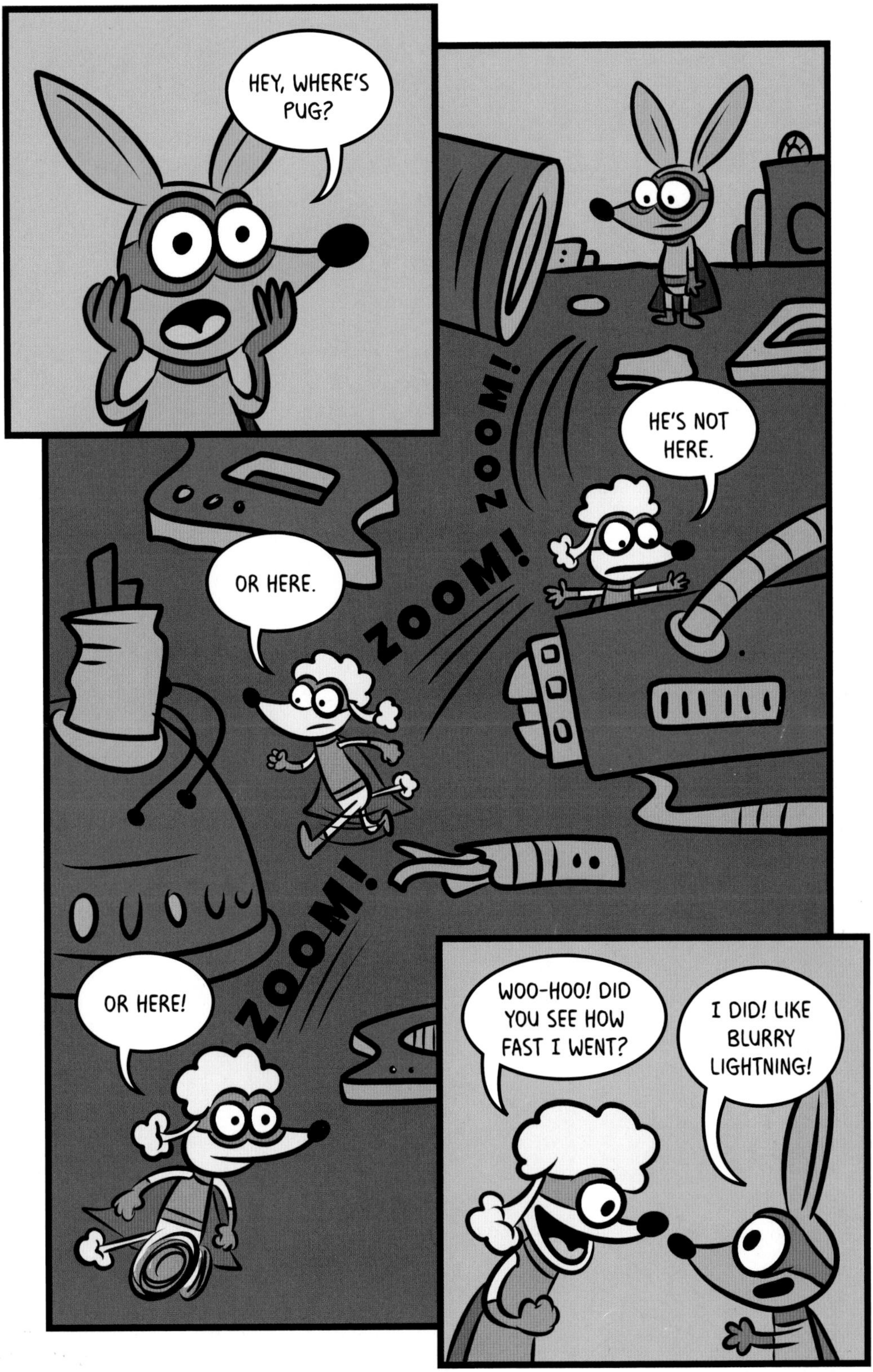
HEY, WHERE'S PUG?
HE'S NOT HERE.
ZOOM! ZOOM!
OR HERE.
ZOOM! ZOOM!
OR HERE!
WOO-HOO! DID YOU SEE HOW FAST I WENT?
I DID! LIKE BLURRY LIGHTNING!

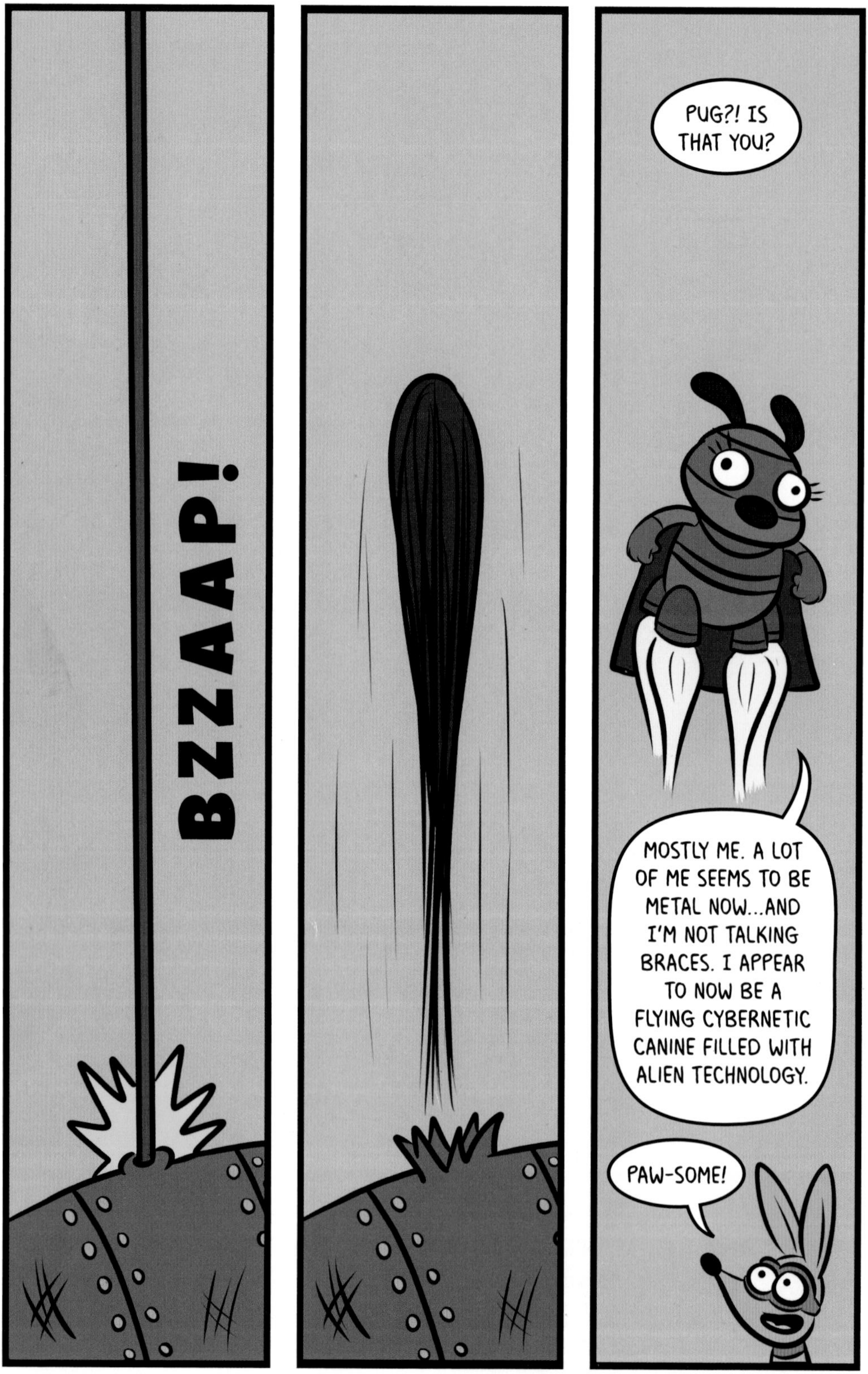
BZZAAP!
PUG?! IS THAT YOU?
MOSTLY ME. A LOT OF ME SEEMS TO BE METAL NOW...AND I'M NOT TALKING BRACES. I APPEAR TO NOW BE A FLYING CYBERNETIC CANINE FILLED WITH ALIEN TECHNOLOGY.
PAW-SOME!

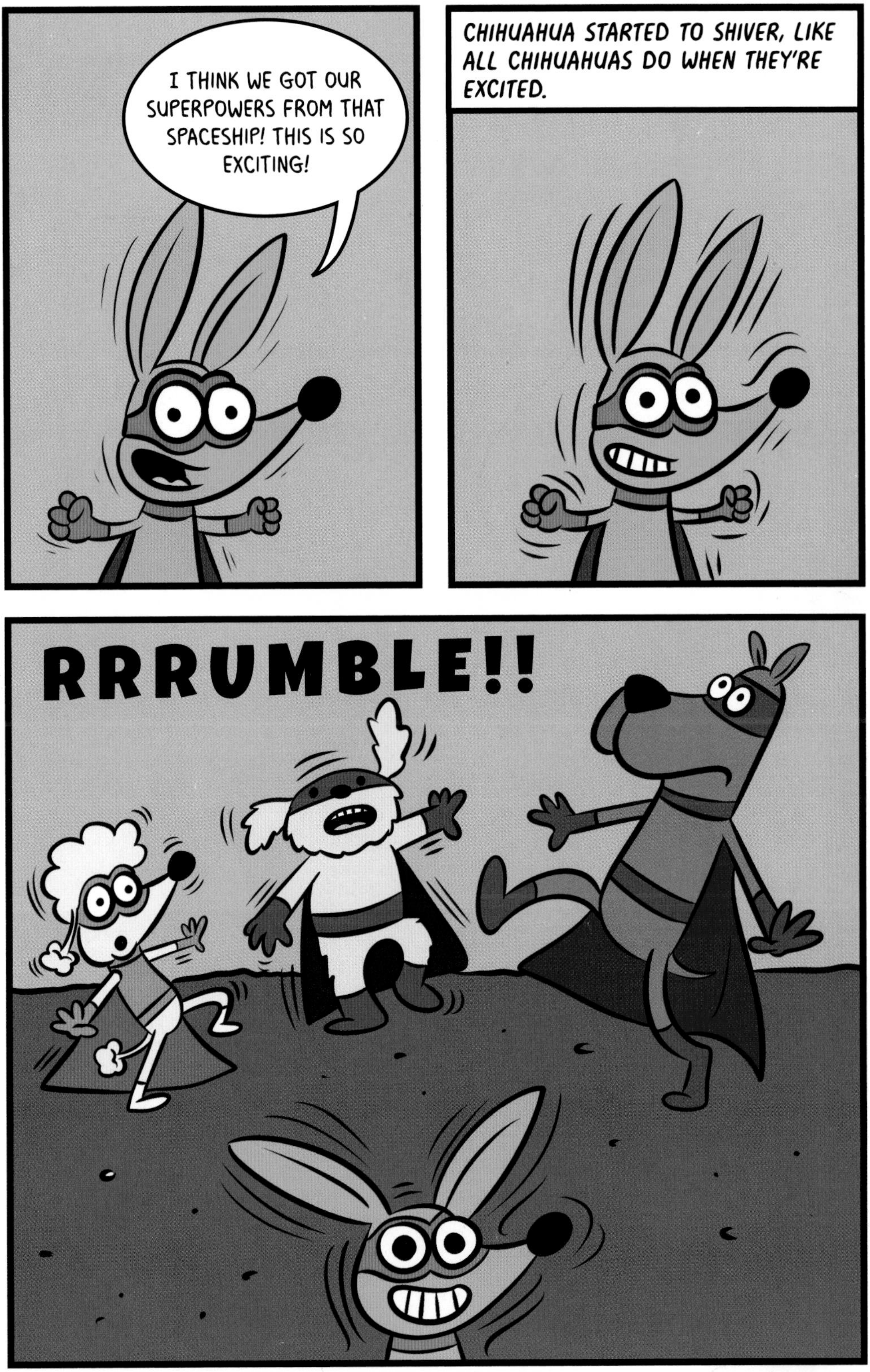
I THINK WE GOT OUR SUPERPOWERS FROM THAT SPACESHIP! THIS IS SO EXCITING!
CHIHUAHUA STARTED TO SHIVER, LIKE ALL CHIHUAHUAS DO WHEN THEY'RE EXCITED.
RRRUMBLE!!

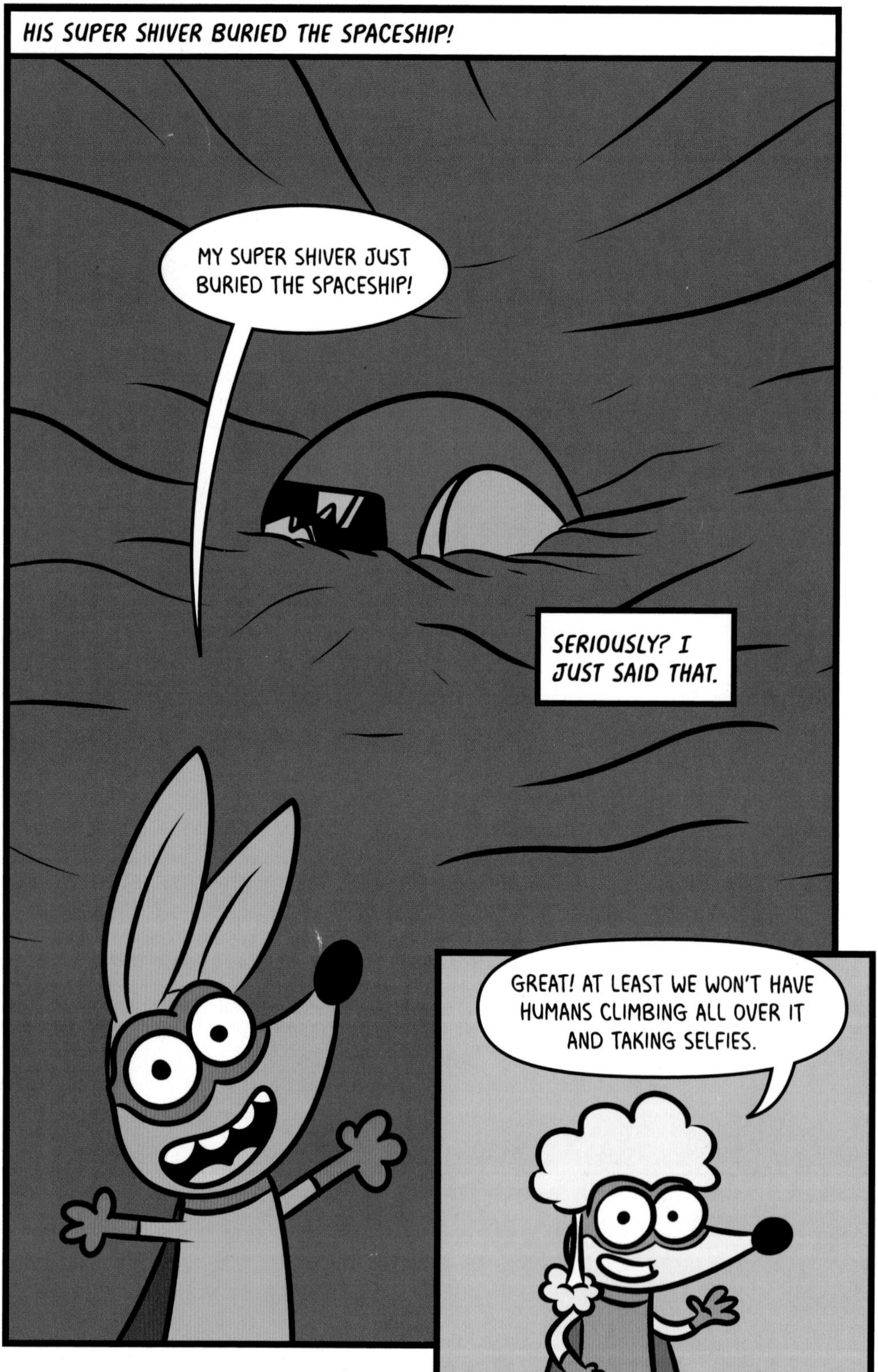
HIS SUPER SHIVER BURIED THE SPACESHIP!
MY SUPER SHIVER JUST BURIED THE SPACESHIP!
SERIOUSLY? I JUST SAID THAT.
GREAT! AT LEAST WE WON'T HAVE HUMANS CLIMBING ALL OVER IT AND TAKING SELFIES.

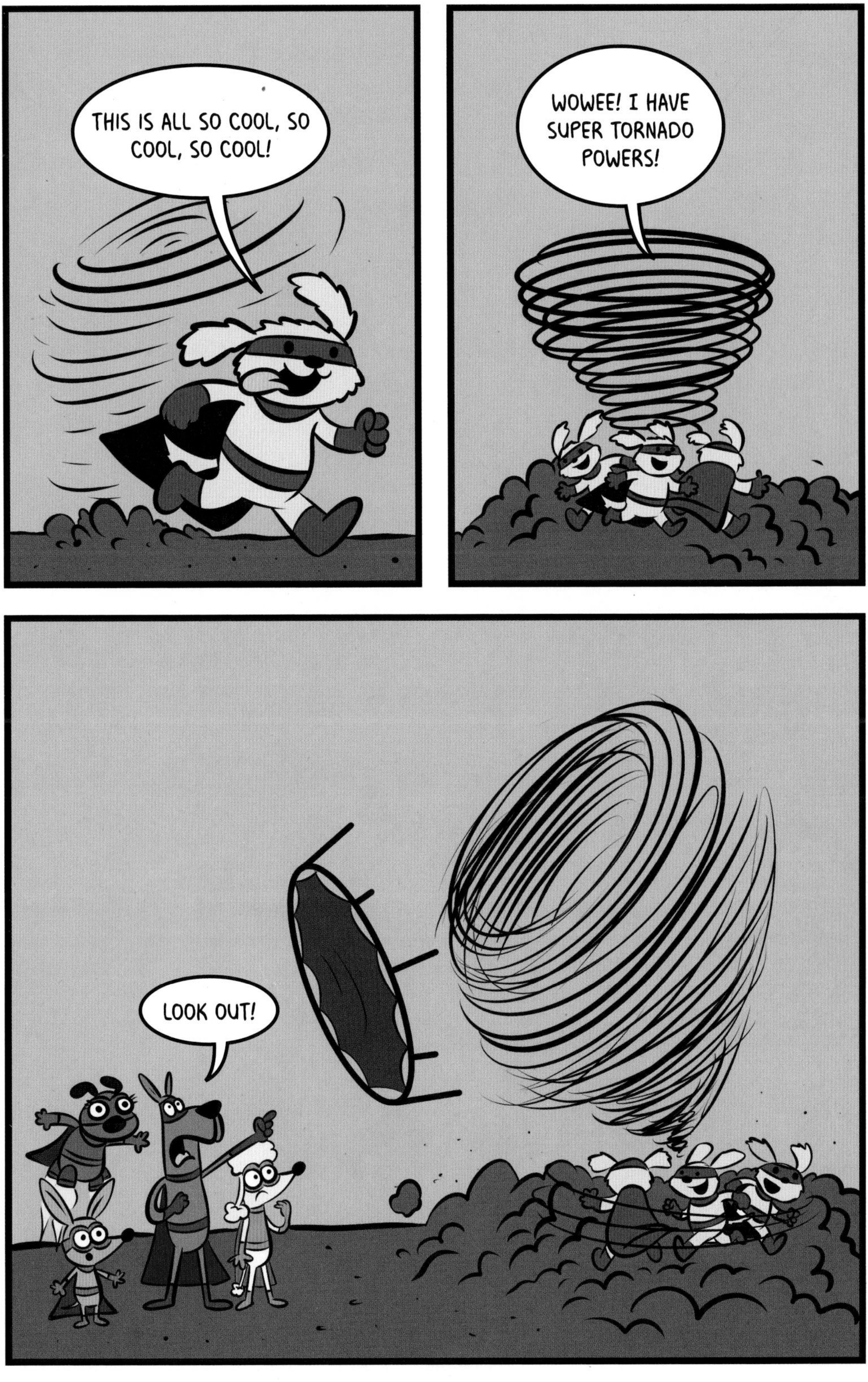
THIS IS ALL SO COOL, SO COOL, SO COOL!
WOWEE! I HAVE SUPER TORNADO POWERS!
LOOK OUT!

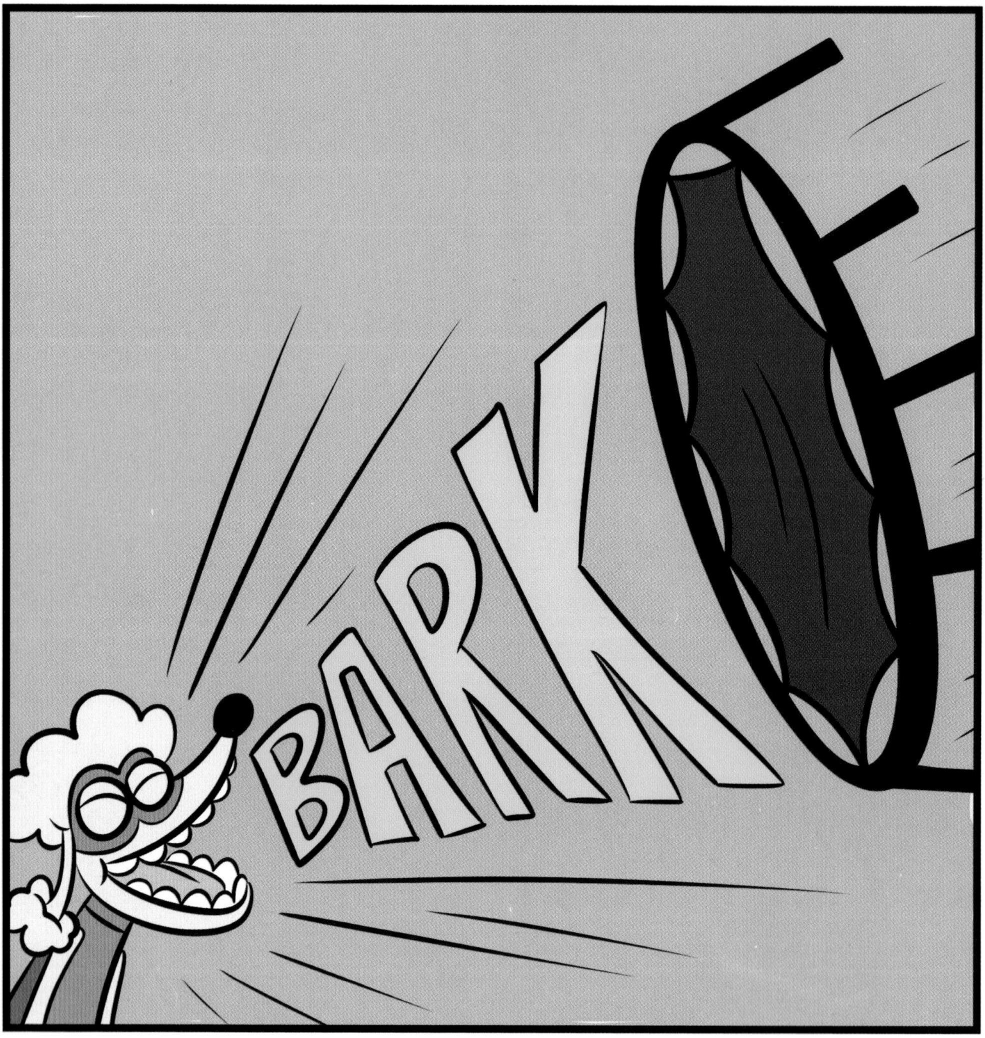
BARK

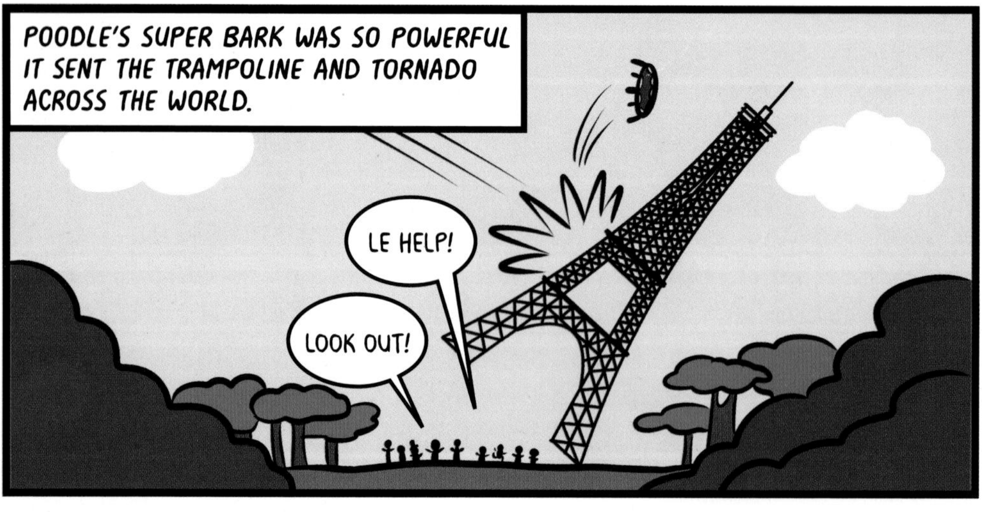
POODLE'S SUPER BARK WAS SO POWERFUL IT SENT THE TRAMPOLINE AND TORNADO ACROSS THE WORLD.
LE HELP!
LOOK OUT!

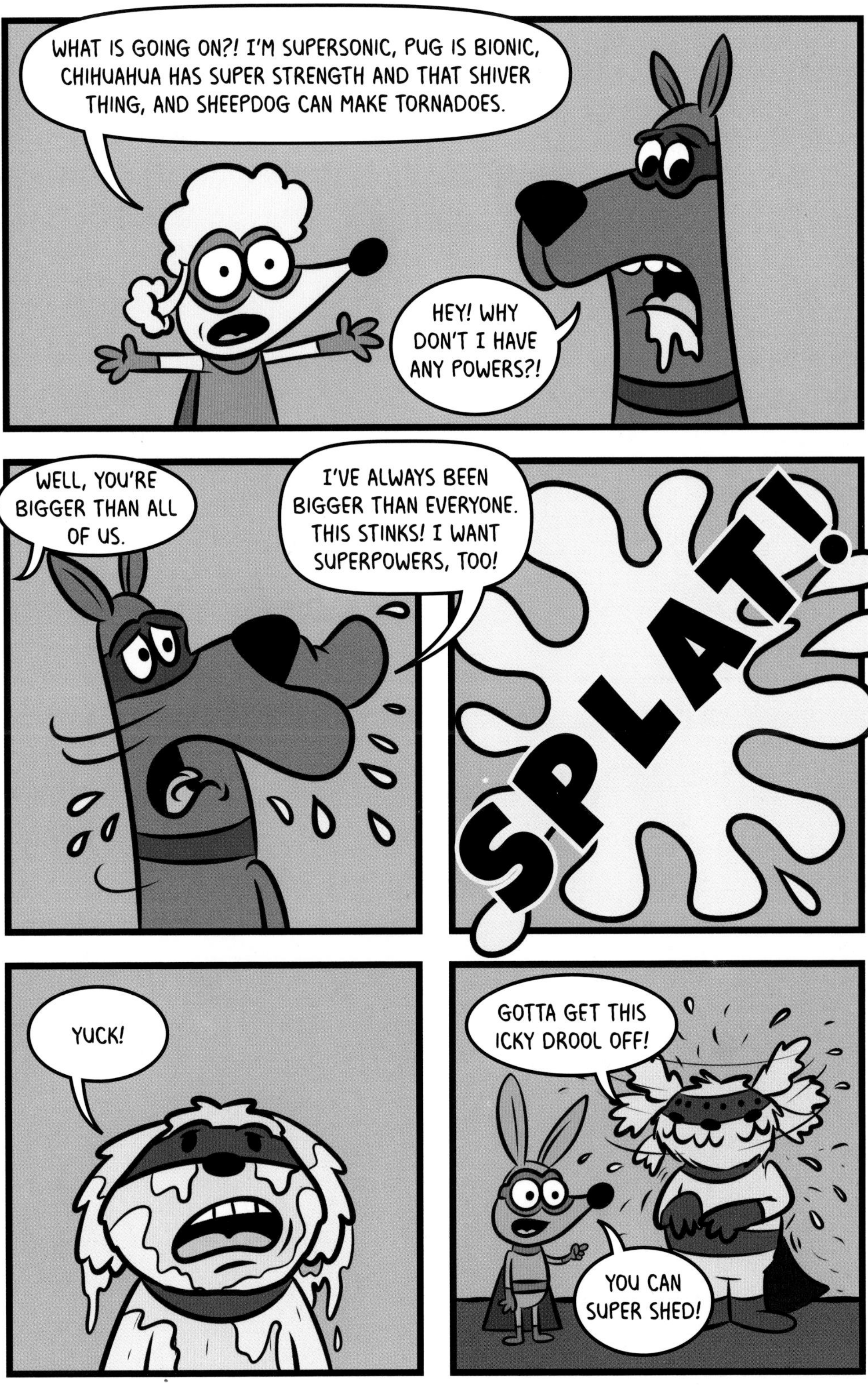

WHAT IS GOING ON?! I'M SUPERSONIC, PUG IS BIONIC, CHIHUAHUA HAS SUPER STRENGTH AND THAT SHIVER THING, AND SHEEPDOG CAN MAKE TORNADOES.
HEY! WHY DON'T I HAVE ANY POWERS?!
WELL, YOU'RE BIGGER THAN ALL OF US.
I'VE ALWAYS BEEN BIGGER THAN EVERYONE. THIS STINKS! I WANT SUPERPOWERS, TOO!
SPLAT!
YUCK!
GOTTA GET THIS ICKY DROOL OFF!
YOU CAN SUPER SHED!

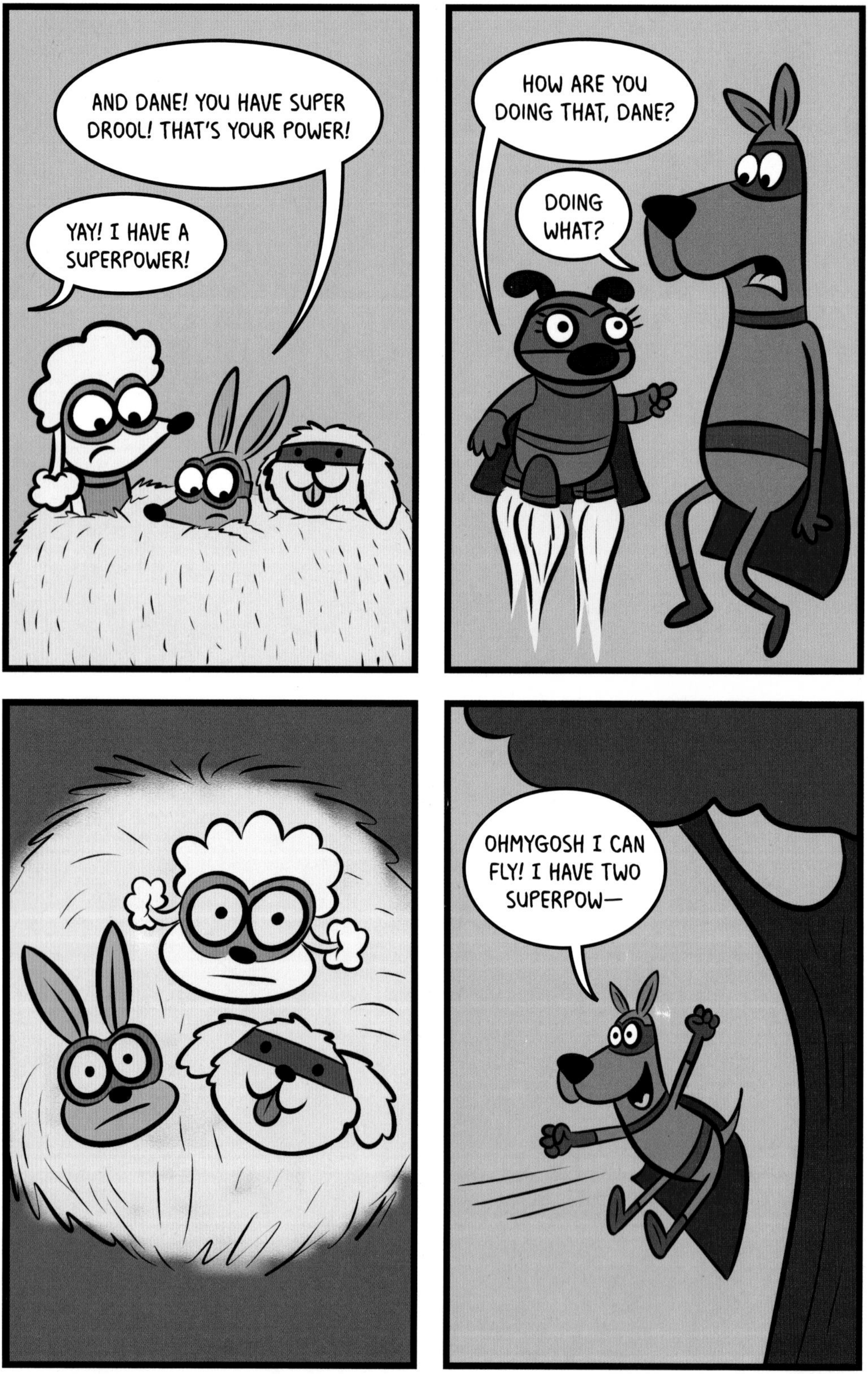
AND DANE! YOU HAVE SUPER DROOL! THAT'S YOUR POWER!
YAY! I HAVE A SUPERPOWER!
HOW ARE YOU DOING THAT, DANE?
DOING WHAT?
OHMYGOSH I CAN FLY! I HAVE TWO SUPERPOW—

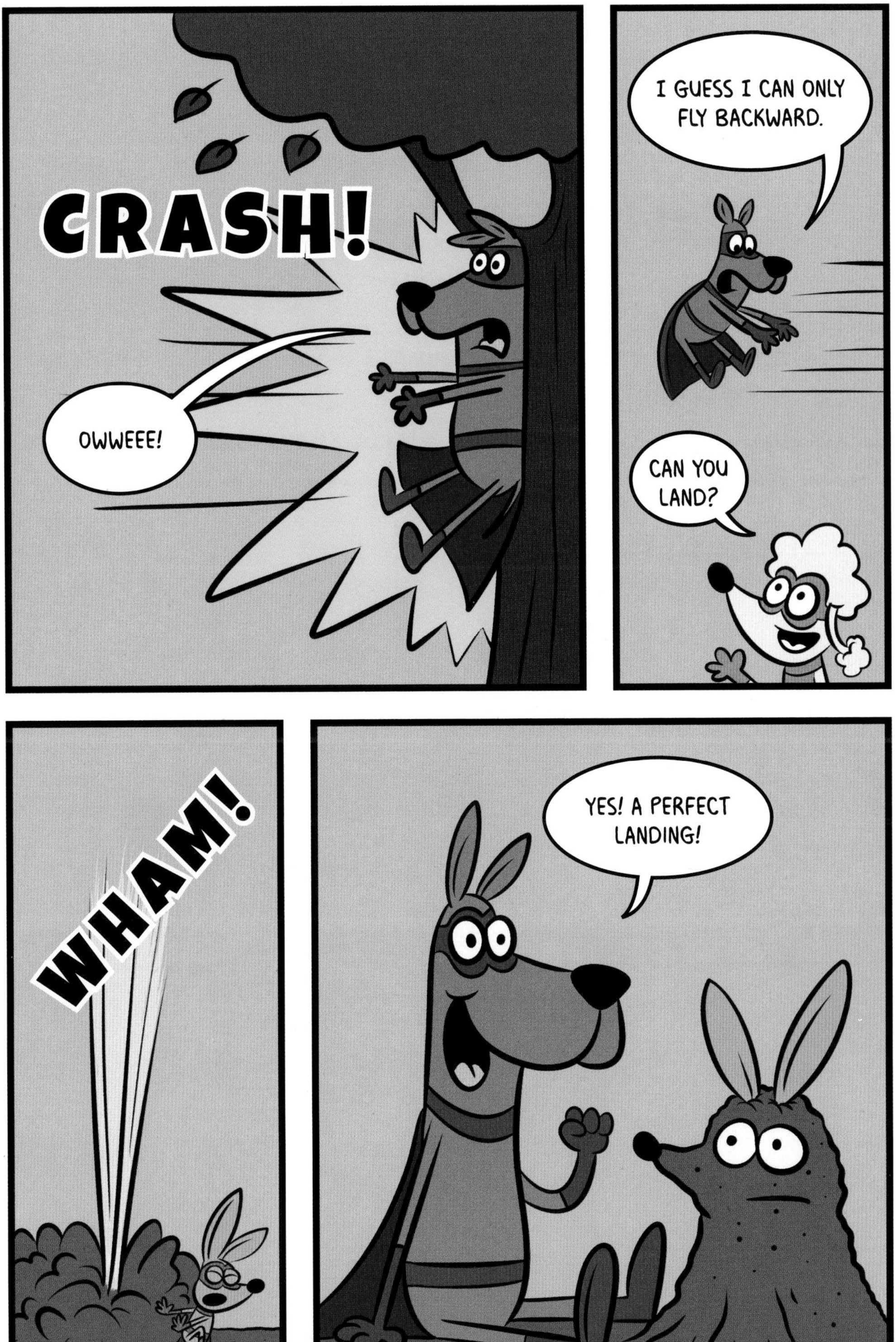
CRASH!
OWWEEE!
I GUESS I CAN ONLY FLY BACKWARD.
CAN YOU LAND?
WHAM!
YES! A PERFECT LANDING!

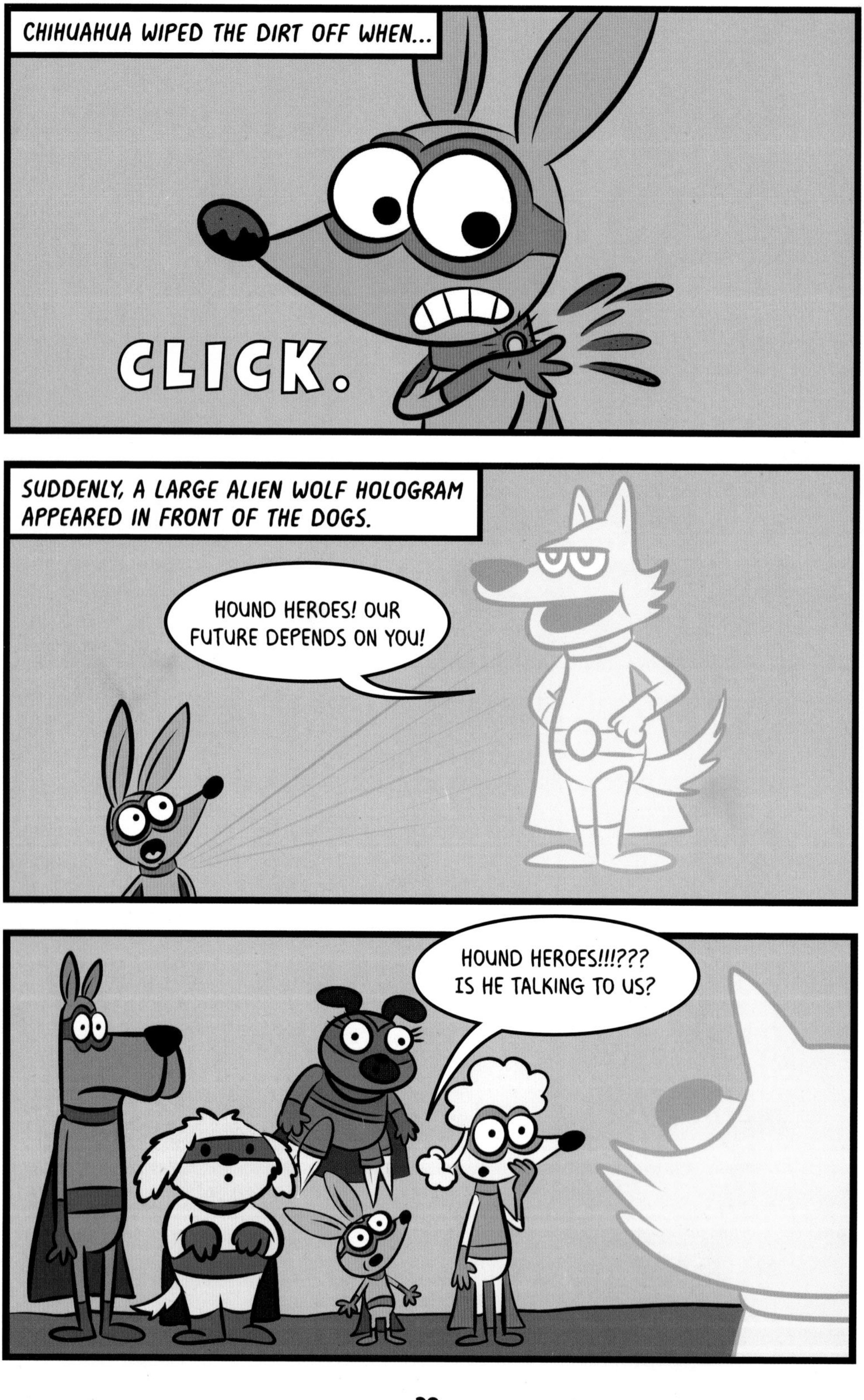
CHIHUAHUA WIPED THE DIRT OFF WHEN...
CLICK.
SUDDENLY, A LARGE ALIEN WOLF HOLOGRAM APPEARED IN FRONT OF THE DOGS.
HOUND HEROES! OUR FUTURE DEPENDS ON YOU!
HOUND HEROES!!!??? IS HE TALKING TO US?

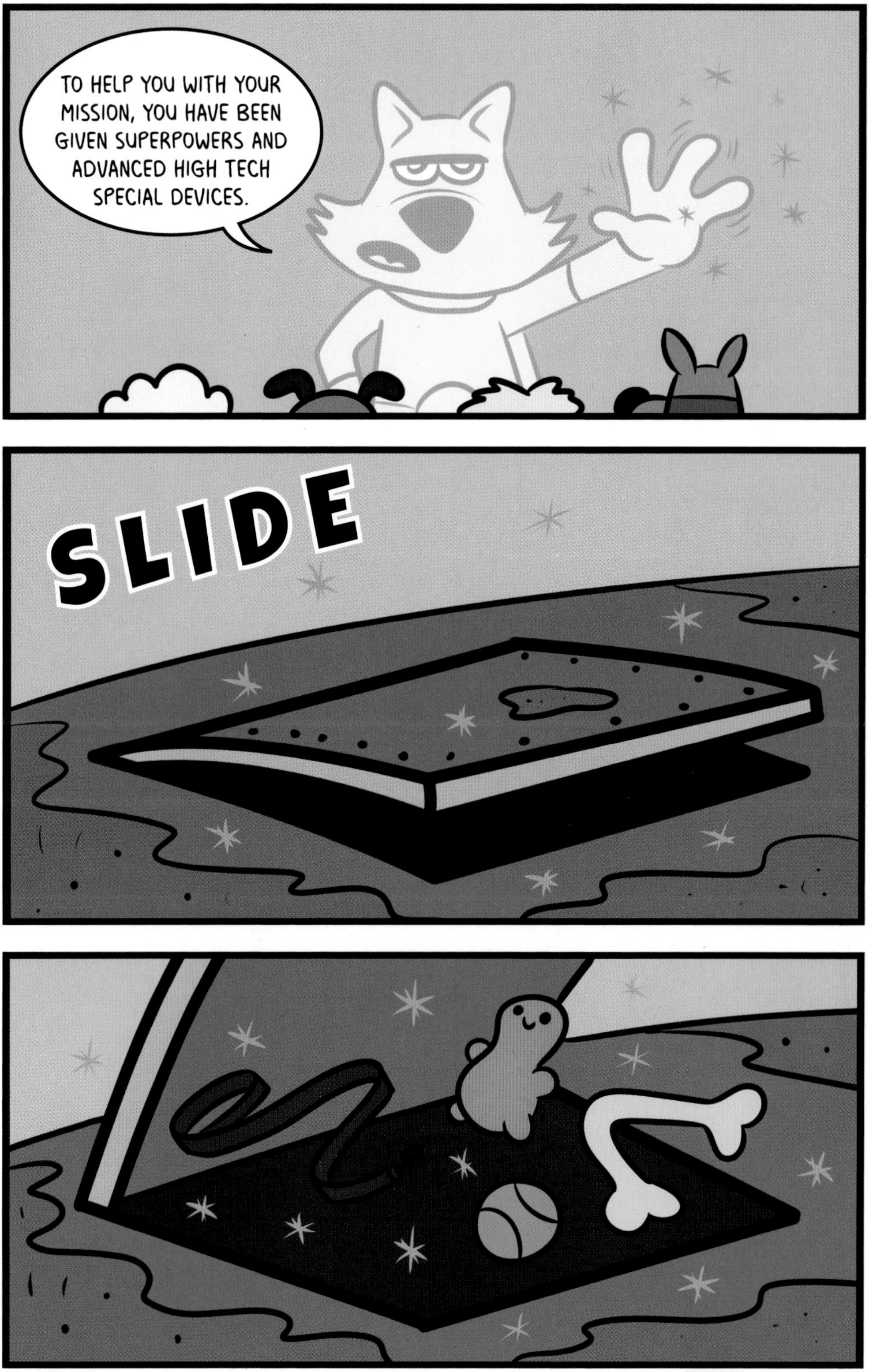
TO HELP YOU WITH YOUR MISSION, YOU HAVE BEEN GIVEN SUPERPOWERS AND ADVANCED HIGH TECH SPECIAL DEVICES.
SLIDE

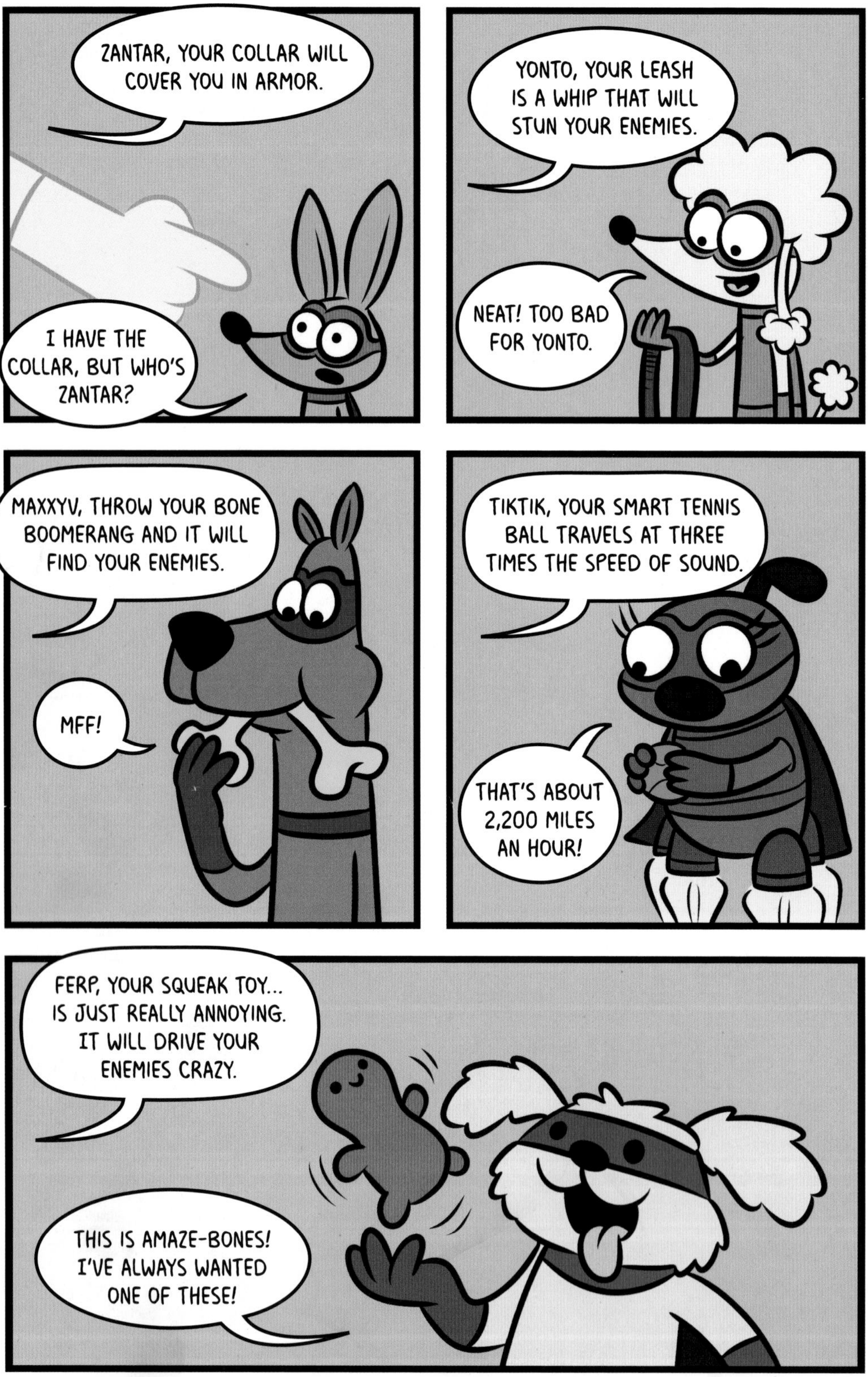
ZANTAR, YOUR COLLAR WILL COVER YOU IN ARMOR.
I HAVE THE COLLAR, BUT WHO'S ZANTAR?
YONTO, YOUR LEASH IS A WHIP THAT WILL STUN YOUR ENEMIES.
NEAT! TOO BAD FOR YONTO.
MAXXYV, THROW YOUR BONE BOOMERANG AND IT WILL FIND YOUR ENEMIES.
MFF!
TIKTIK, YOUR SMART TENNIS BALL TRAVELS AT THREE TIMES THE SPEED OF SOUND.
THAT'S ABOUT 2,200 MILES AN HOUR!
FERP, YOUR SQUEAK TOY... IS JUST REALLY ANNOYING. IT WILL DRIVE YOUR ENEMIES CRAZY.
THIS IS AMAZE-BONES! I'VE ALWAYS WANTED ONE OF THESE!

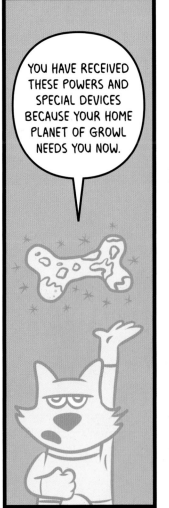

AND WITH THAT, THE HOLOGRAM DISAPPEARED.

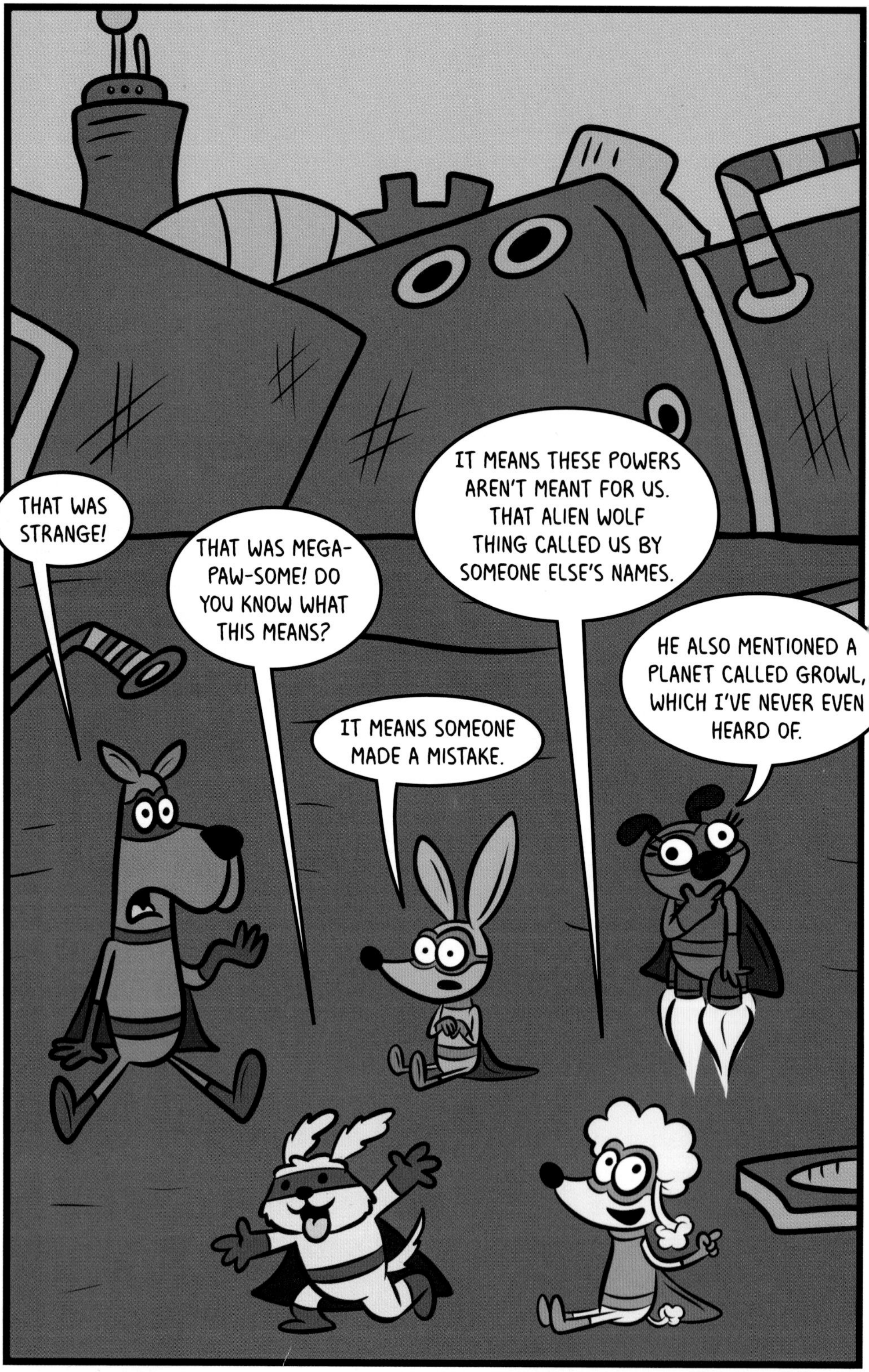
THAT WAS STRANGE!
THAT WAS MEGA-PAW-SOME! DO YOU KNOW WHAT THIS MEANS?
IT MEANS THESE POWERS AREN'T MEANT FOR US. THAT ALIEN WOLF THING CALLED US BY SOMEONE ELSE'S NAMES.
IT MEANS SOMEONE MADE A MISTAKE.
HE ALSO MENTIONED A PLANET CALLED GROWL, WHICH I'VE NEVER EVEN HEARD OF.

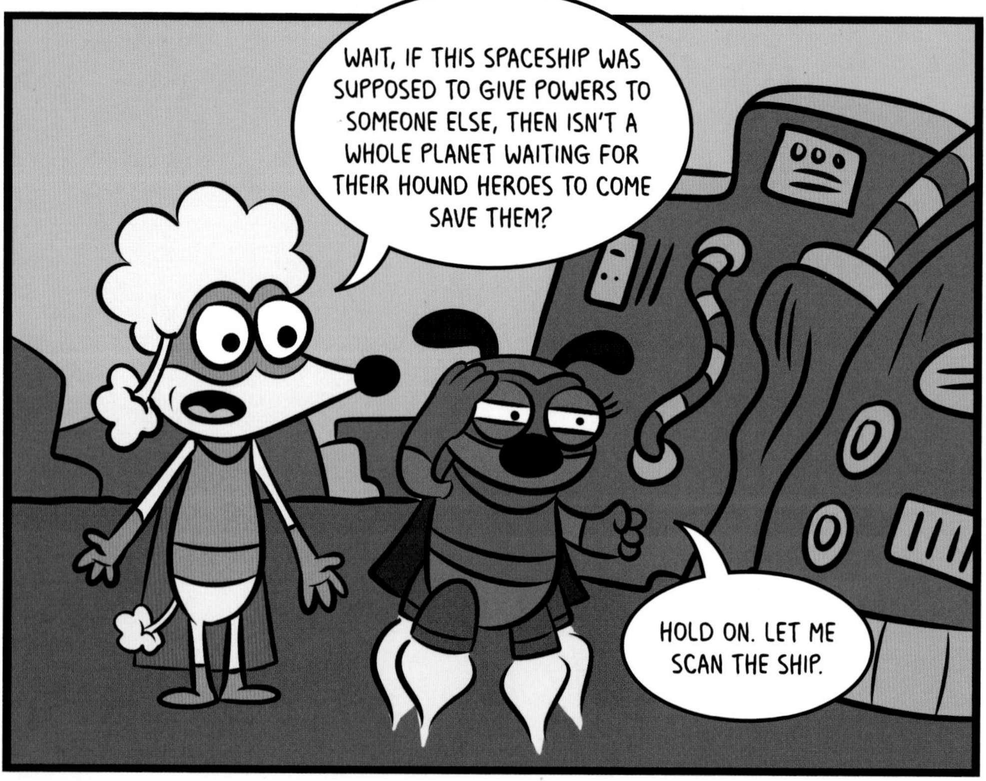
WAIT, IF THIS SPACESHIP WAS SUPPOSED TO GIVE POWERS TO SOMEONE ELSE, THEN ISN'T A WHOLE PLANET WAITING FOR THEIR HOUND HEROES TO COME SAVE THEM?
HOLD ON. LET ME SCAN THE SHIP.

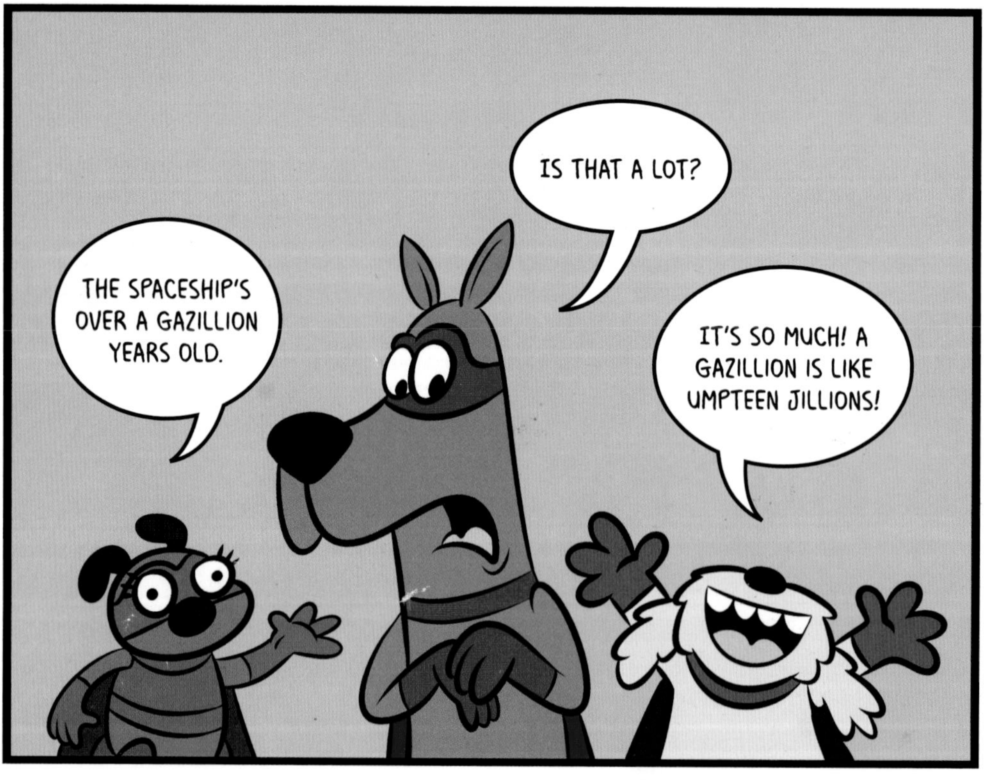
THE SPACESHIP'S OVER A GAZILLION YEARS OLD.
IS THAT A LOT?
IT'S SO MUCH! A GAZILLION IS LIKE UMPTEEN JILLIONS!

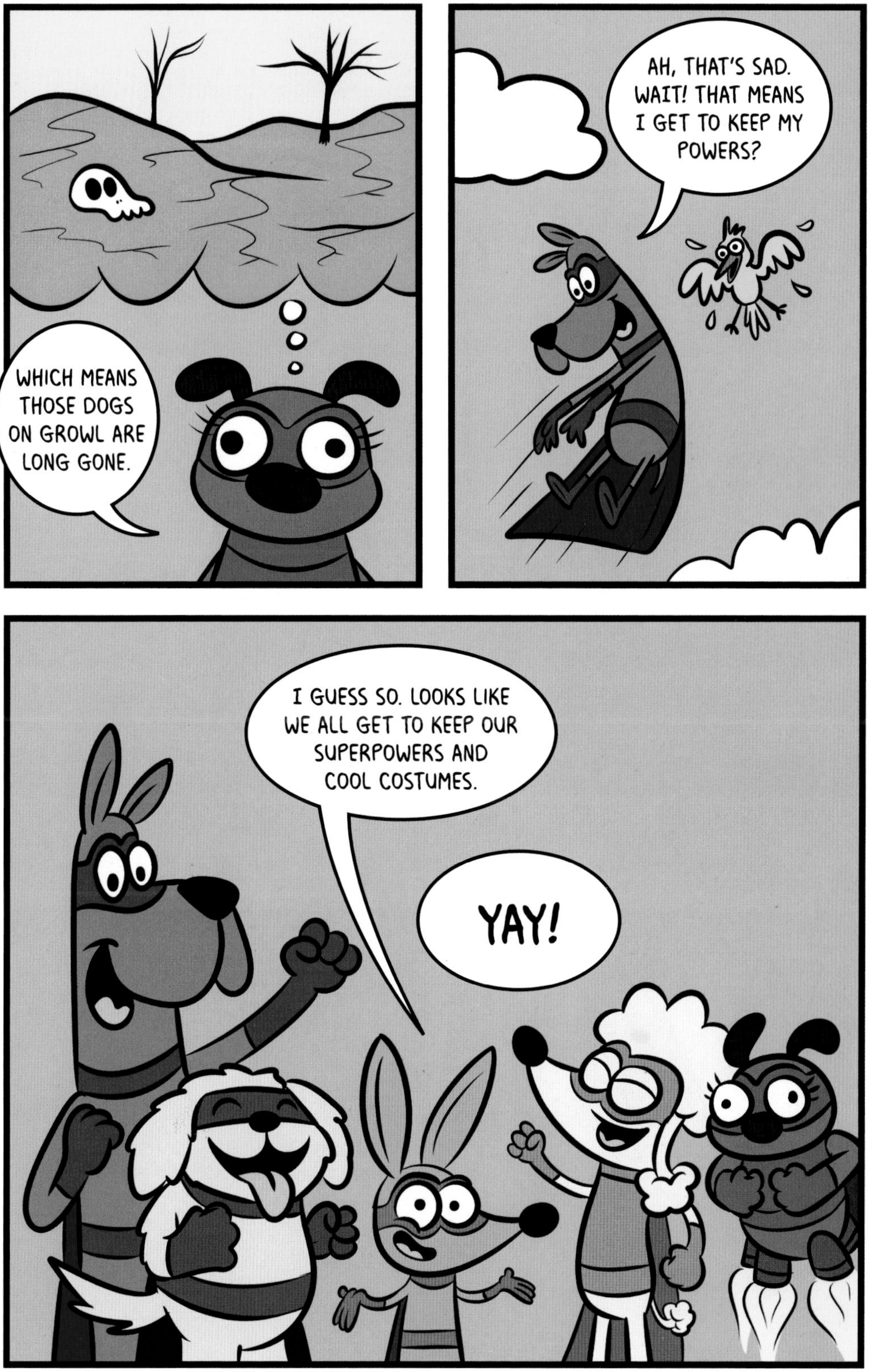
WHICH MEANS THOSE DOGS ON GROWL ARE LONG GONE.
AH, THAT'S SAD. WAIT! THAT MEANS I GET TO KEEP MY POWERS?
I GUESS SO. LOOKS LIKE WE ALL GET TO KEEP OUR SUPERPOWERS AND COOL COSTUMES.
YAY!

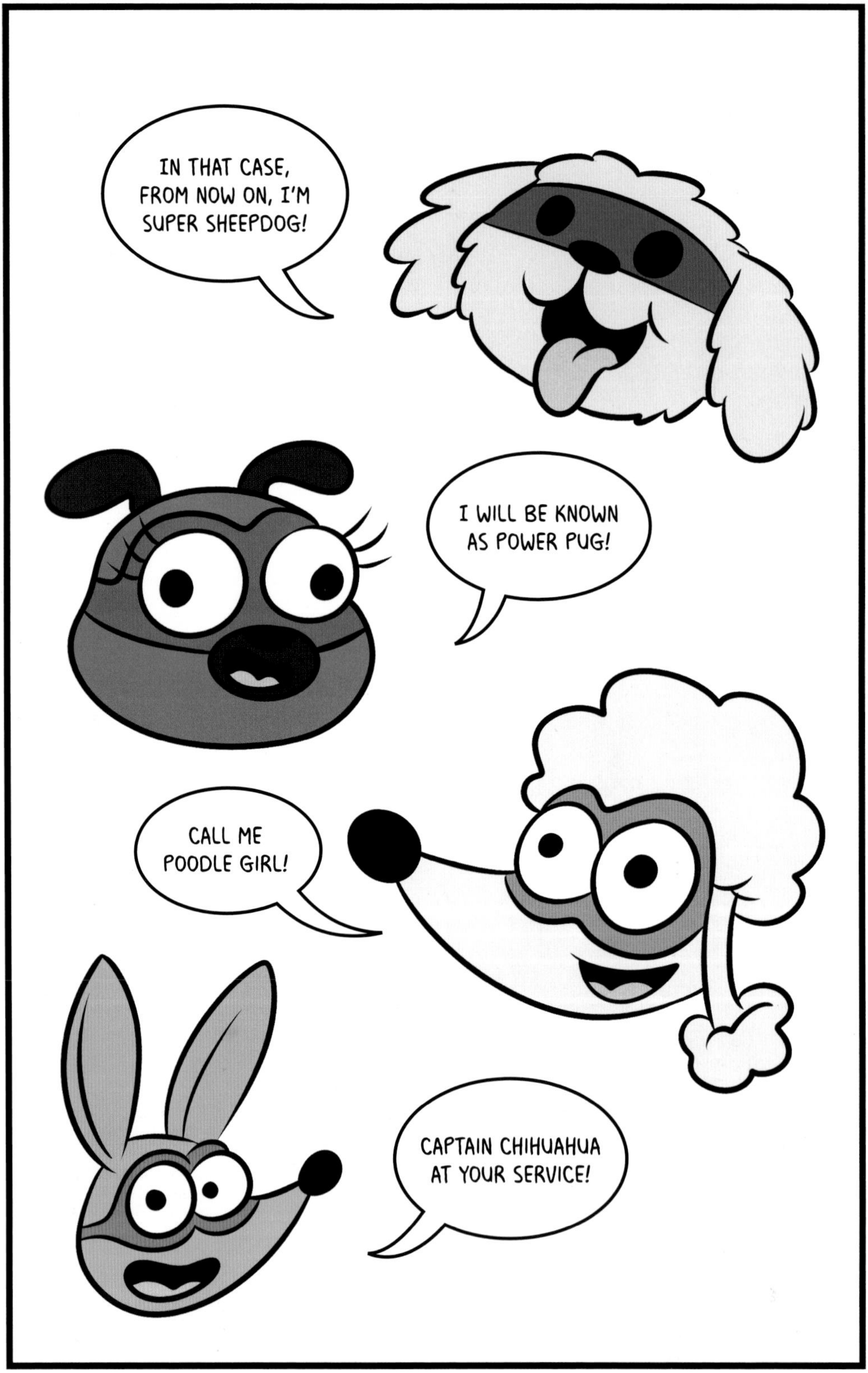
IN THAT CASE, FROM NOW ON, I'M SUPER SHEEPDOG!
I WILL BE KNOWN AS POWER PUG!
CALL ME POODLE GIRL!
CAPTAIN CHIHUAHUA AT YOUR SERVICE!

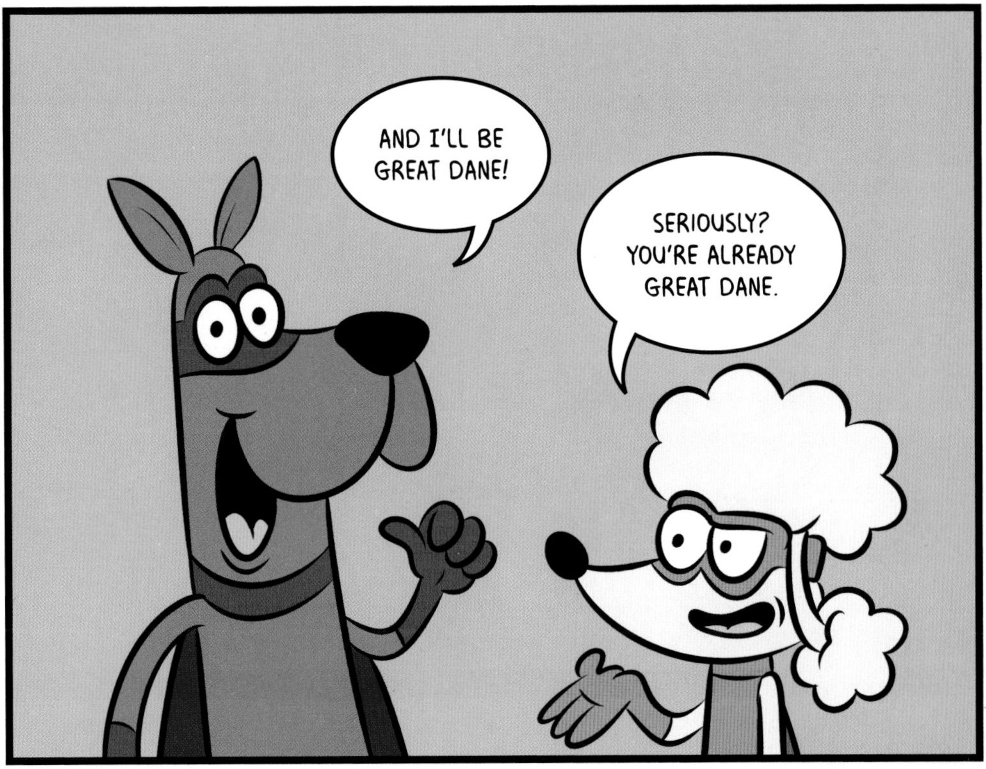
AND I'LL BE GREAT DANE!
SERIOUSLY? YOU'RE ALREADY GREAT DANE.

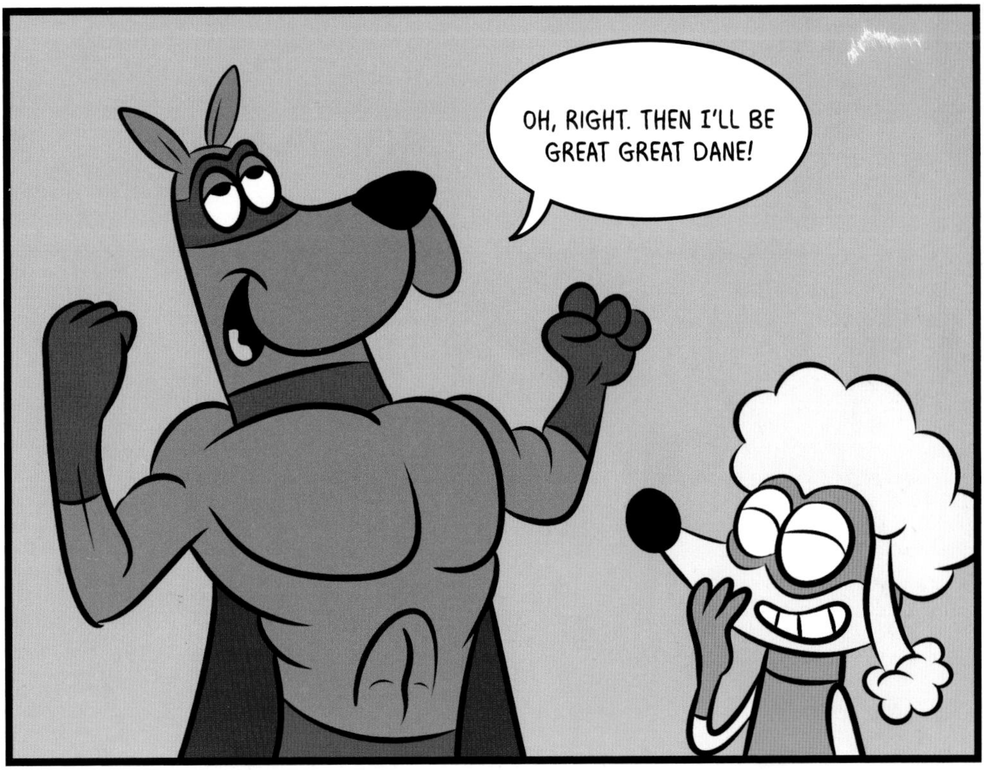
OH, RIGHT. THEN I'LL BE GREAT GREAT DANE!

MEET THE HOUND HEROES!

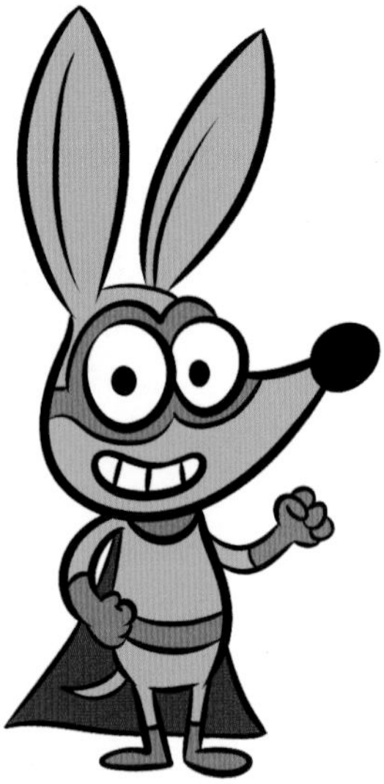

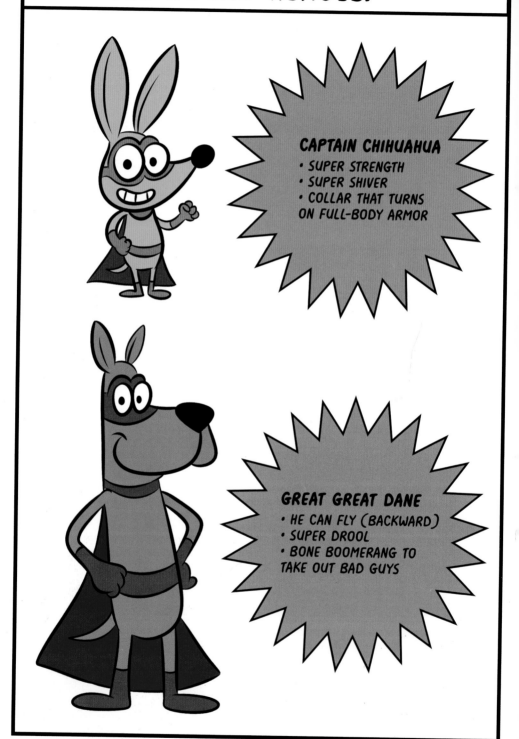

CAPTAIN CHIHUAHUA

- SUPER STRENGTH
- SUPER SHIVER
- COLLAR THAT TURNS ON FULL-BODY ARMOR

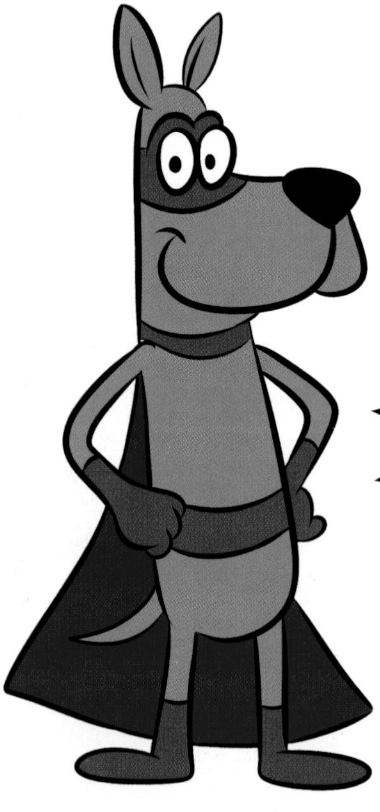

GREAT GREAT DANE

- HE CAN FLY (BACKWARD)
- SUPER DROOL
- BONE BOOMERANG TO TAKE OUT BAD GUYS

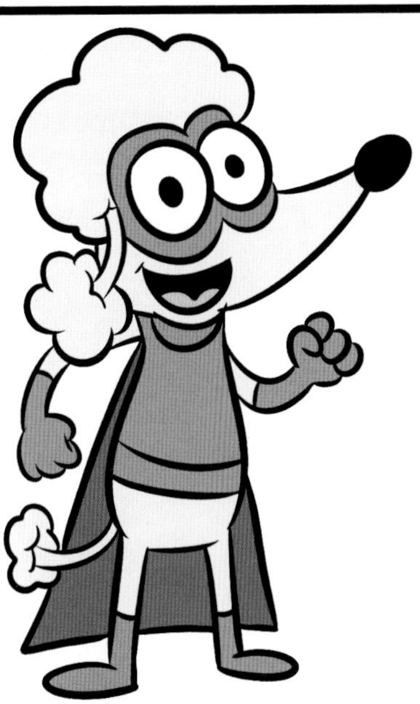

POODLE GIRL
- SUPER SPEED
- SUPER BARK
- WHIP THAT STUNS ENEMIES

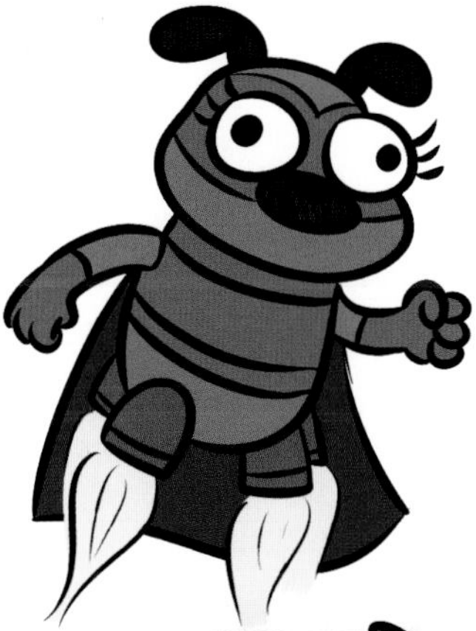

POWER PUG
- CYBERNETIC, FLYING BODY
- LASER EYES
- TENNIS BALL CANNON

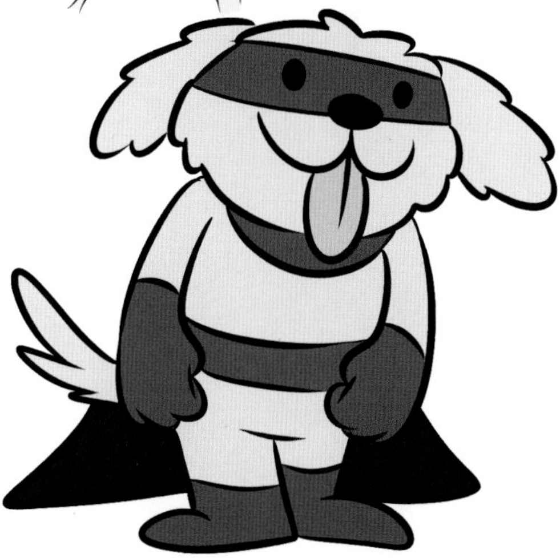

SUPER SHEEPDOG
- TORNADO POWER
- SUPER SHED
- SUPER-ANNOYING SQUEAK TOY

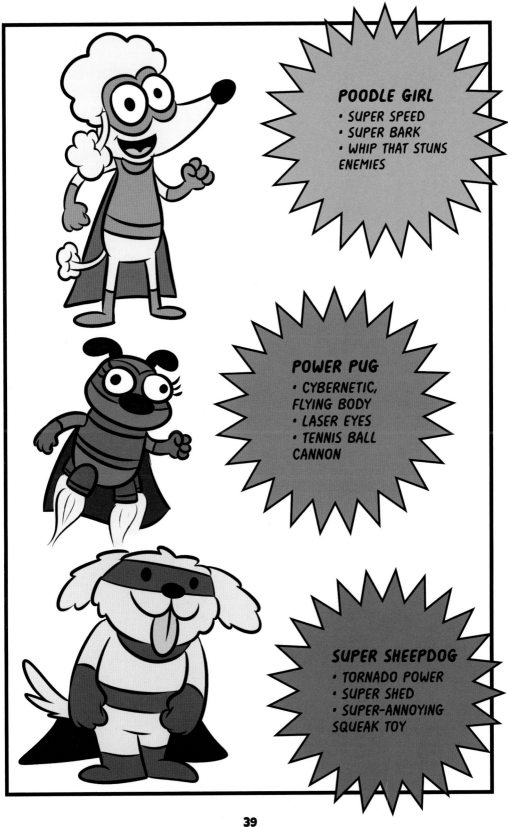

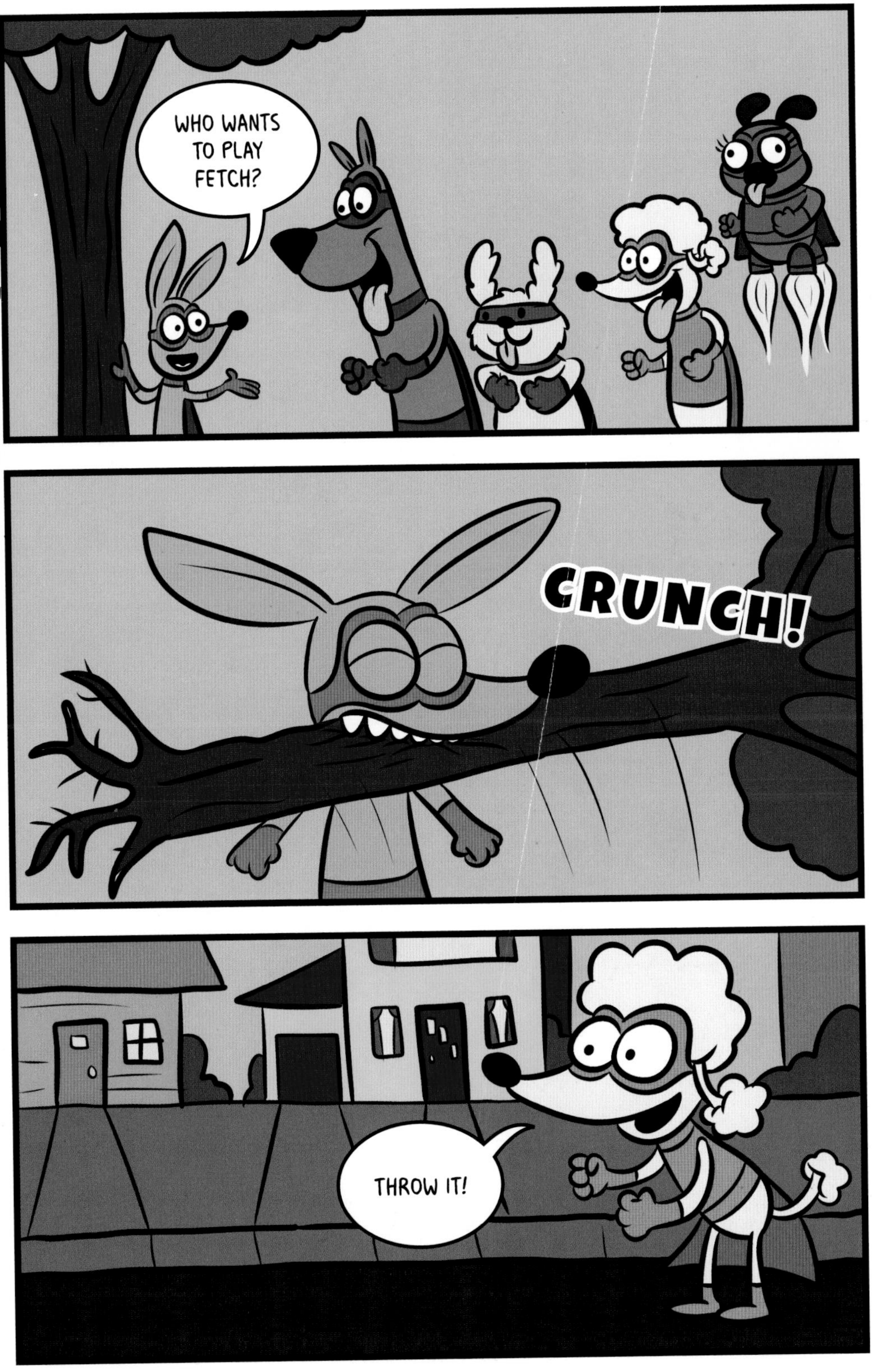
WHO WANTS TO PLAY FETCH?
CRUNCH!
THROW IT!

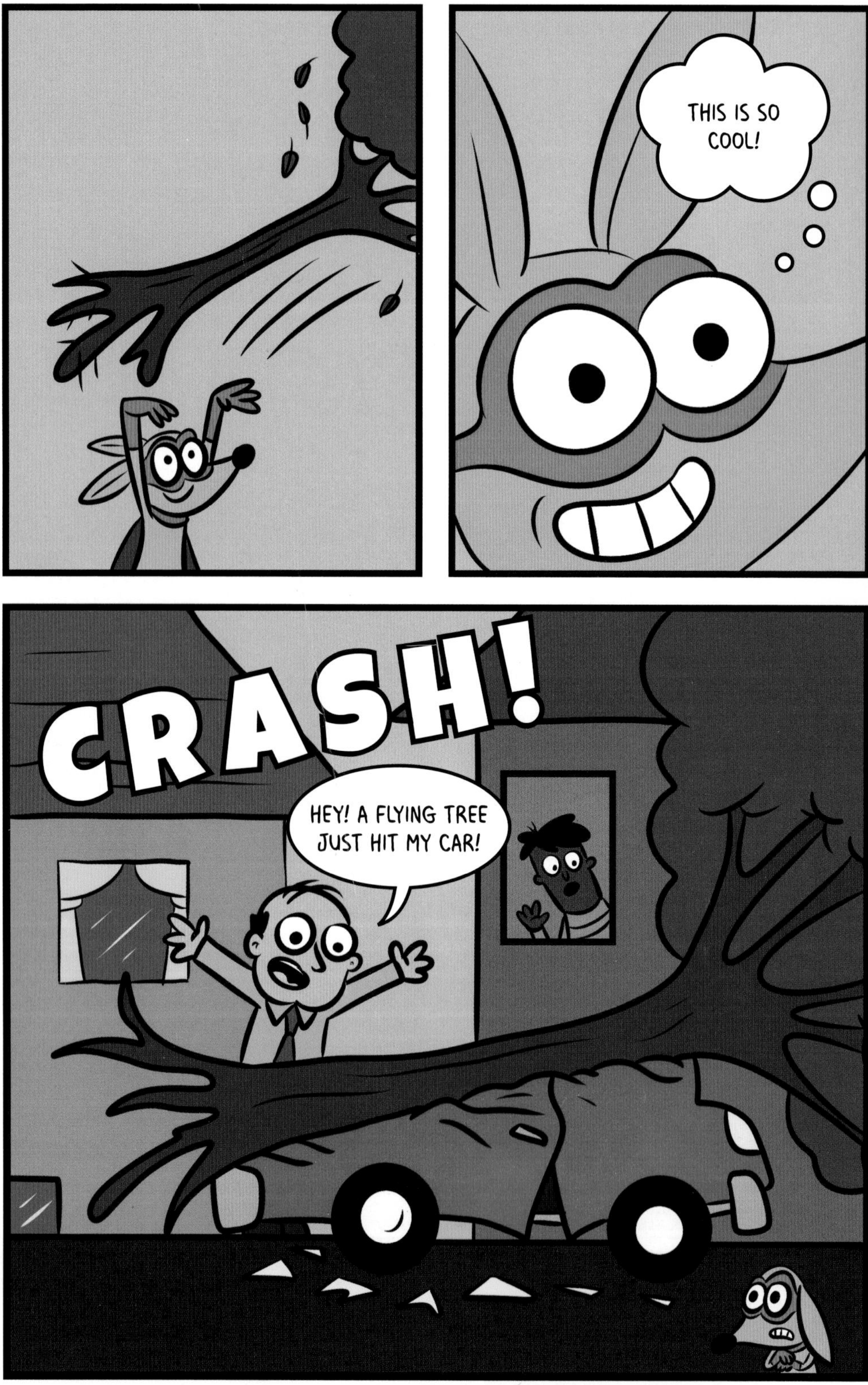
THIS IS SO COOL!
CRASH!
HEY! A FLYING TREE JUST HIT MY CAR!

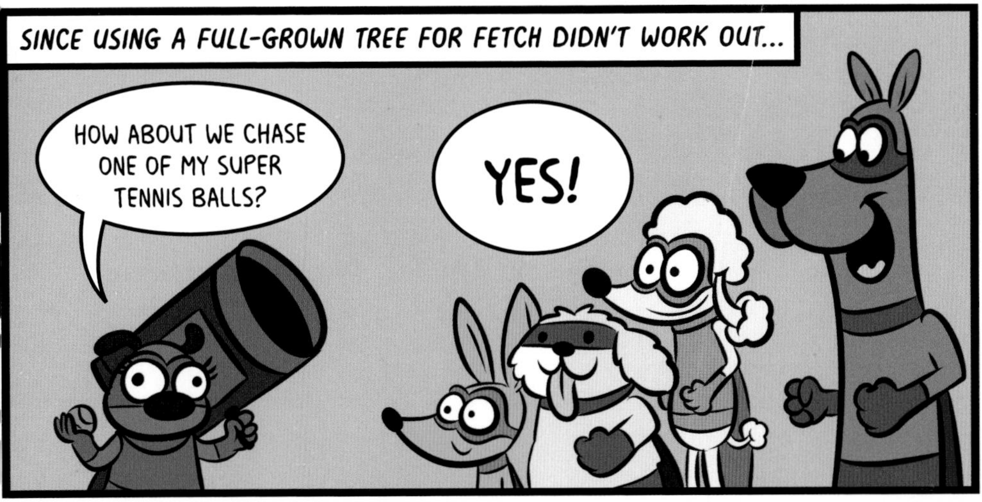
SINCE USING A FULL-GROWN TREE FOR FETCH DIDN'T WORK OUT...
HOW ABOUT WE CHASE ONE OF MY SUPER TENNIS BALLS?
YES!

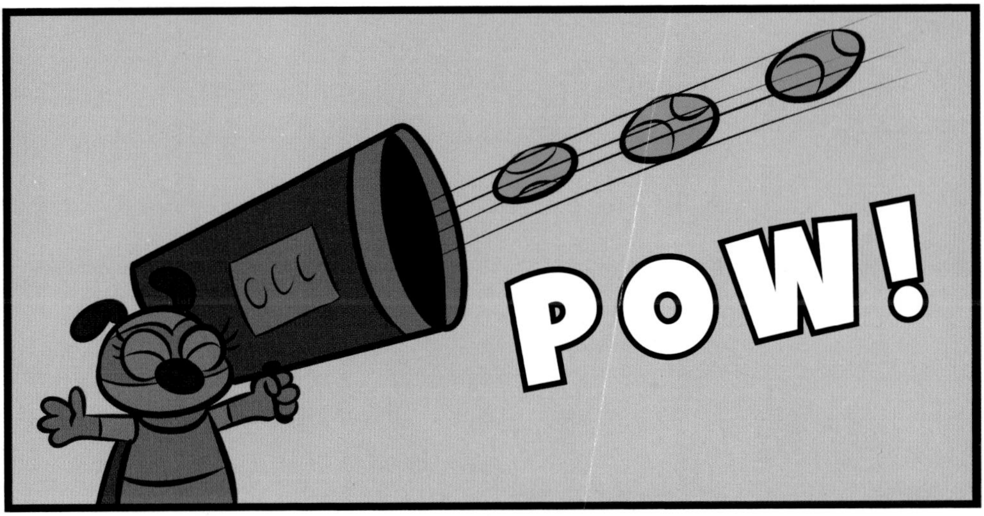
POW!

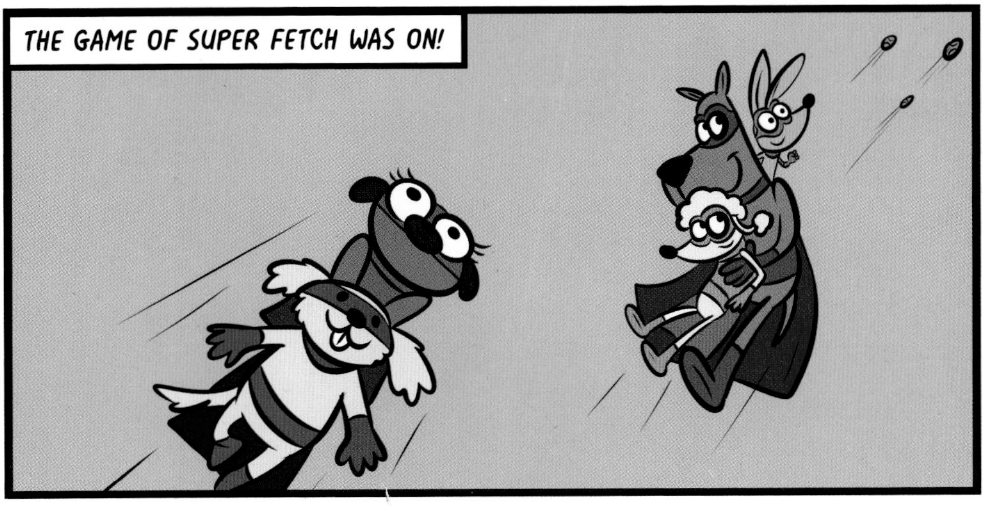
THE GAME OF SUPER FETCH WAS ON!

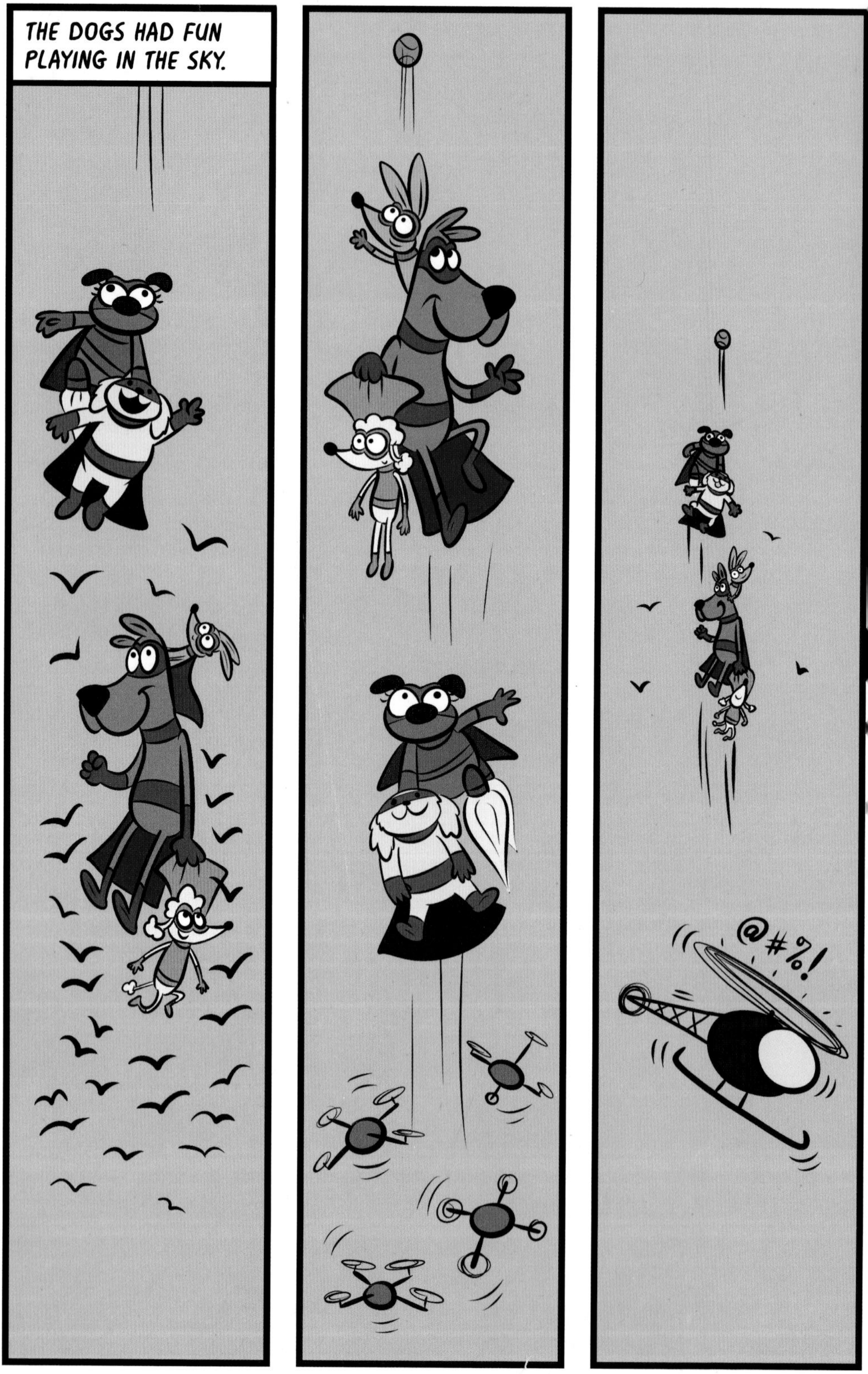
THE DOGS HAD FUN PLAYING IN THE SKY.
@#%!

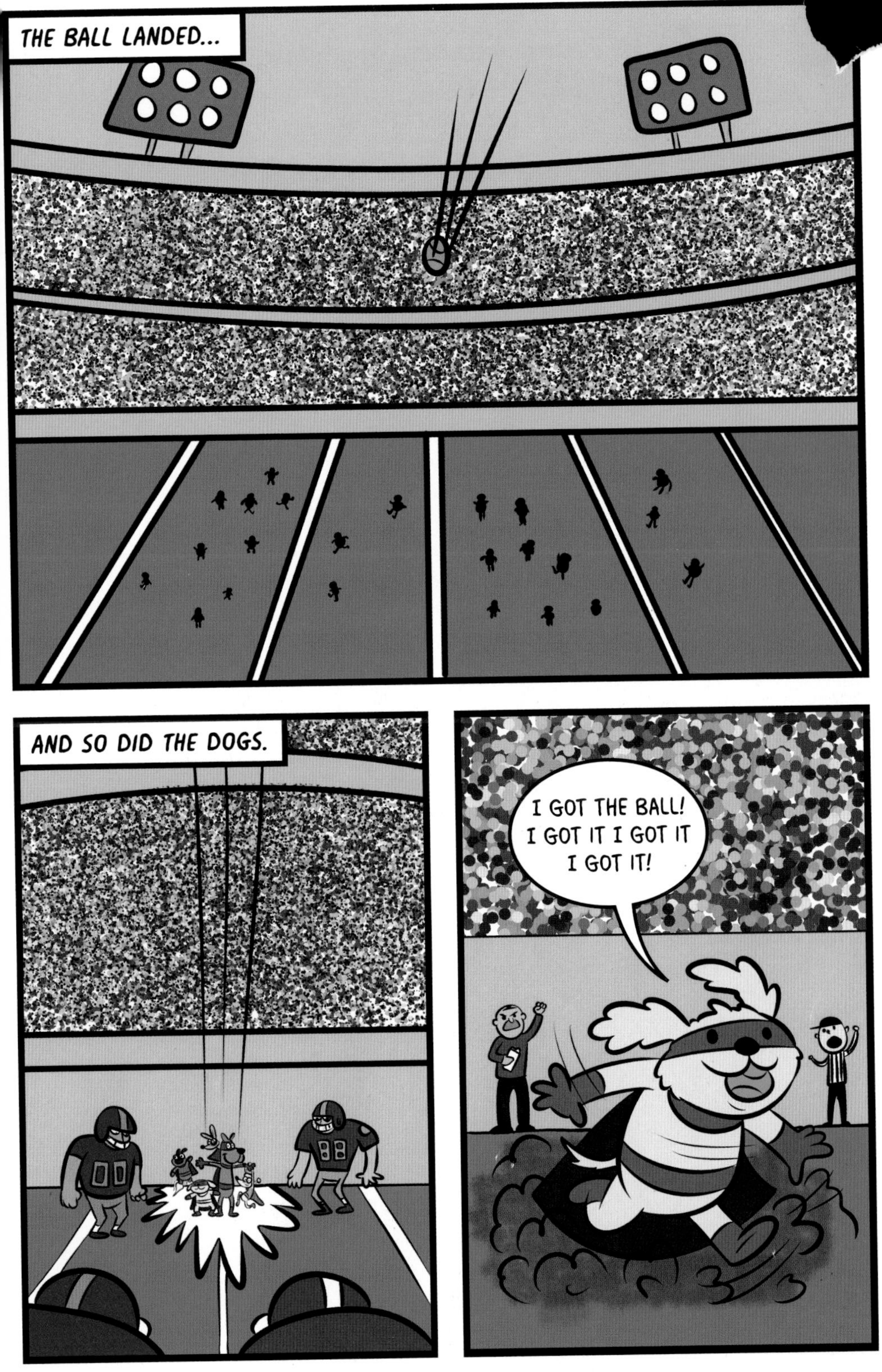
THE BALL LANDED...
AND SO DID THE DOGS.
I GOT THE BALL! I GOT IT I GOT IT I GOT IT!

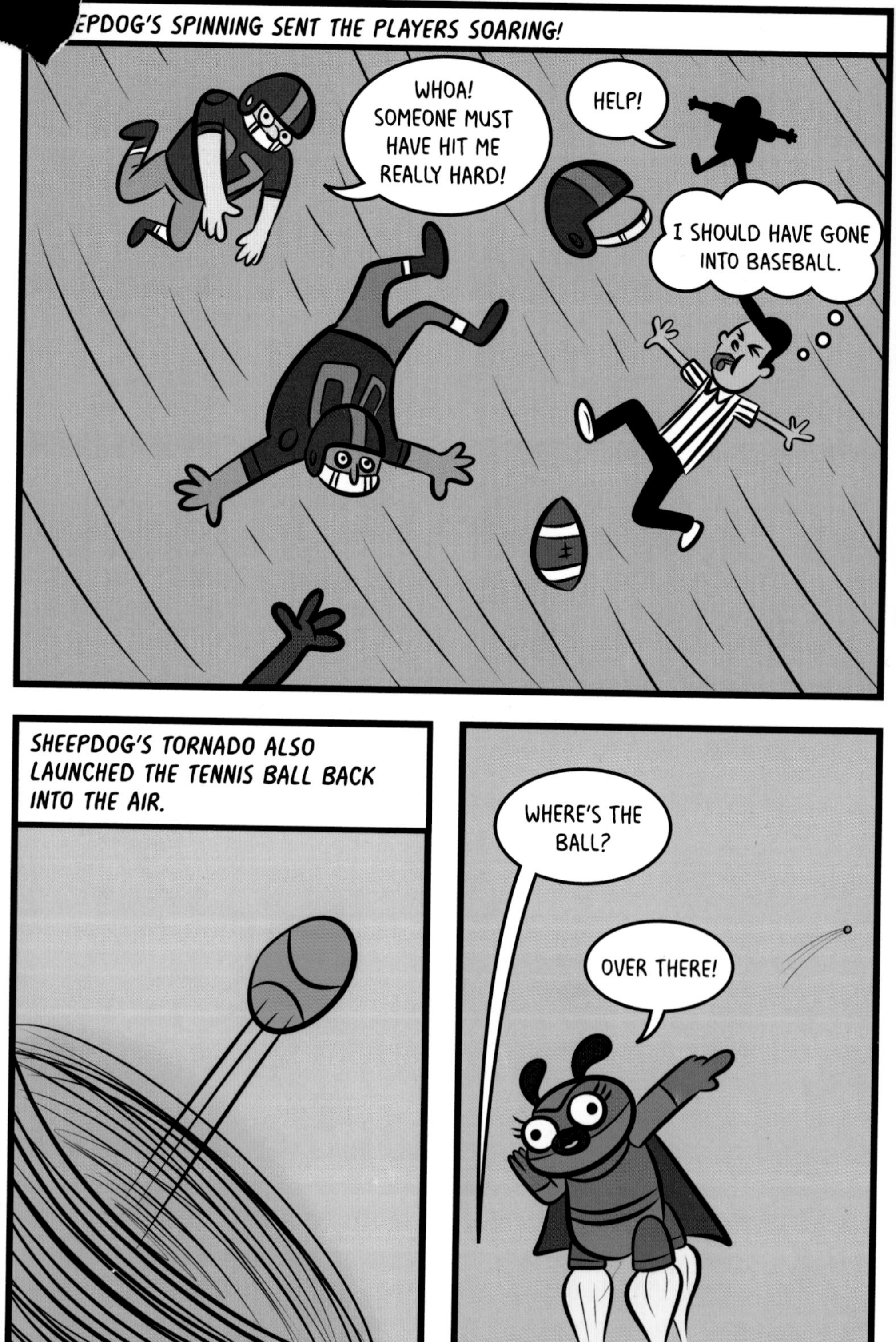
EPDOG'S SPINNING SENT THE PLAYERS SOARING!
WHOA! SOMEONE MUST HAVE HIT ME REALLY HARD!
HELP!
I SHOULD HAVE GONE INTO BASEBALL.
SHEEPDOG'S TORNADO ALSO LAUNCHED THE TENNIS BALL BACK INTO THE AIR.
WHERE'S THE BALL?
OVER THERE!

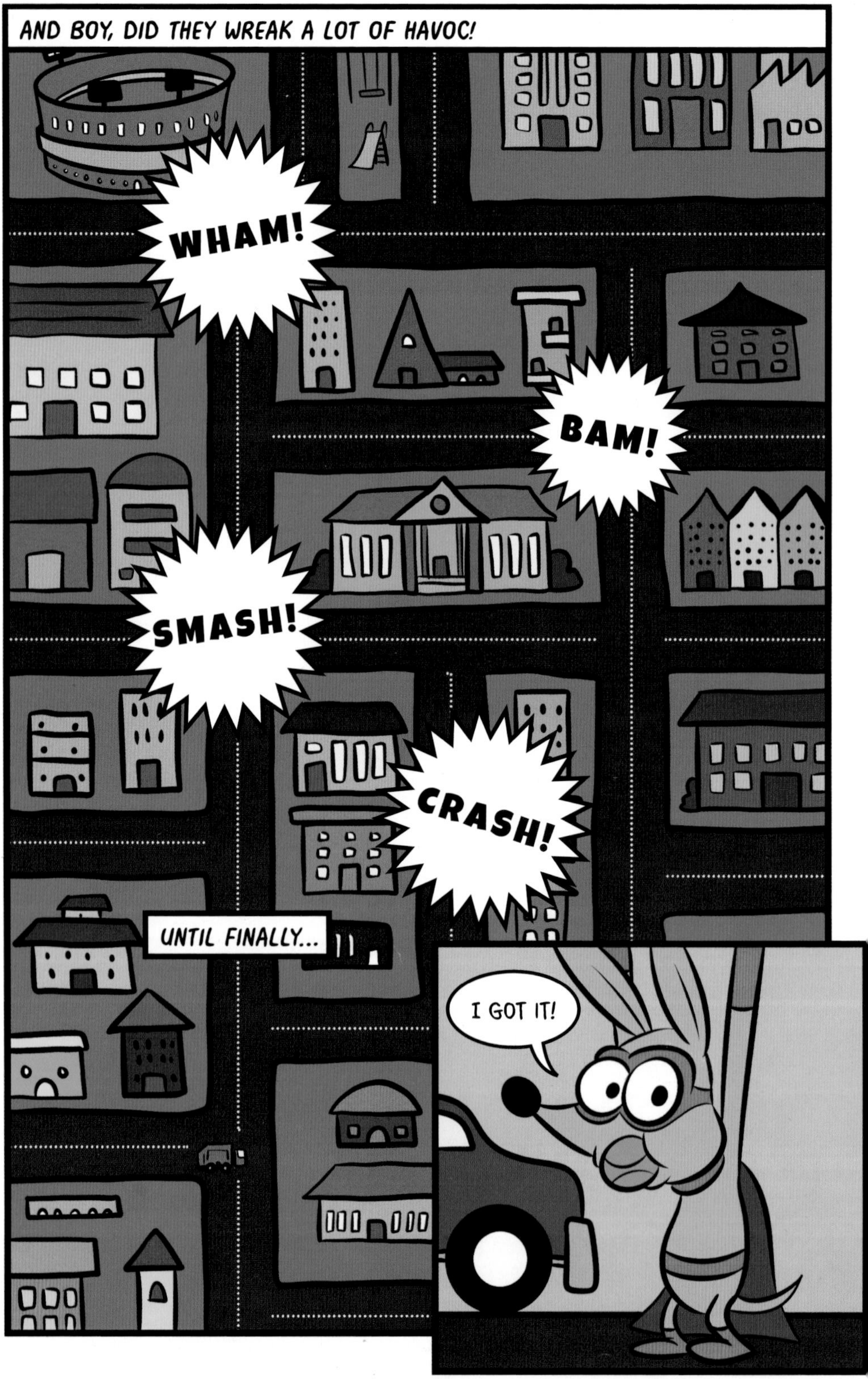
AND BOY, DID THEY WREAK A LOT OF HAVOC!
WHAM!
BAM!
SMASH!
CRASH!
UNTIL FINALLY...
I GOT IT!

THE HOUNDS HAPPILY ROLLED IN CRUSTY GREEN BEANS, ROTTEN FISH, CURDLED MILK, MOLDY BAGELS, AND OTHER SLIMY BLOBS OF STINKY, STICKY, AND ICKY GARBAGE.

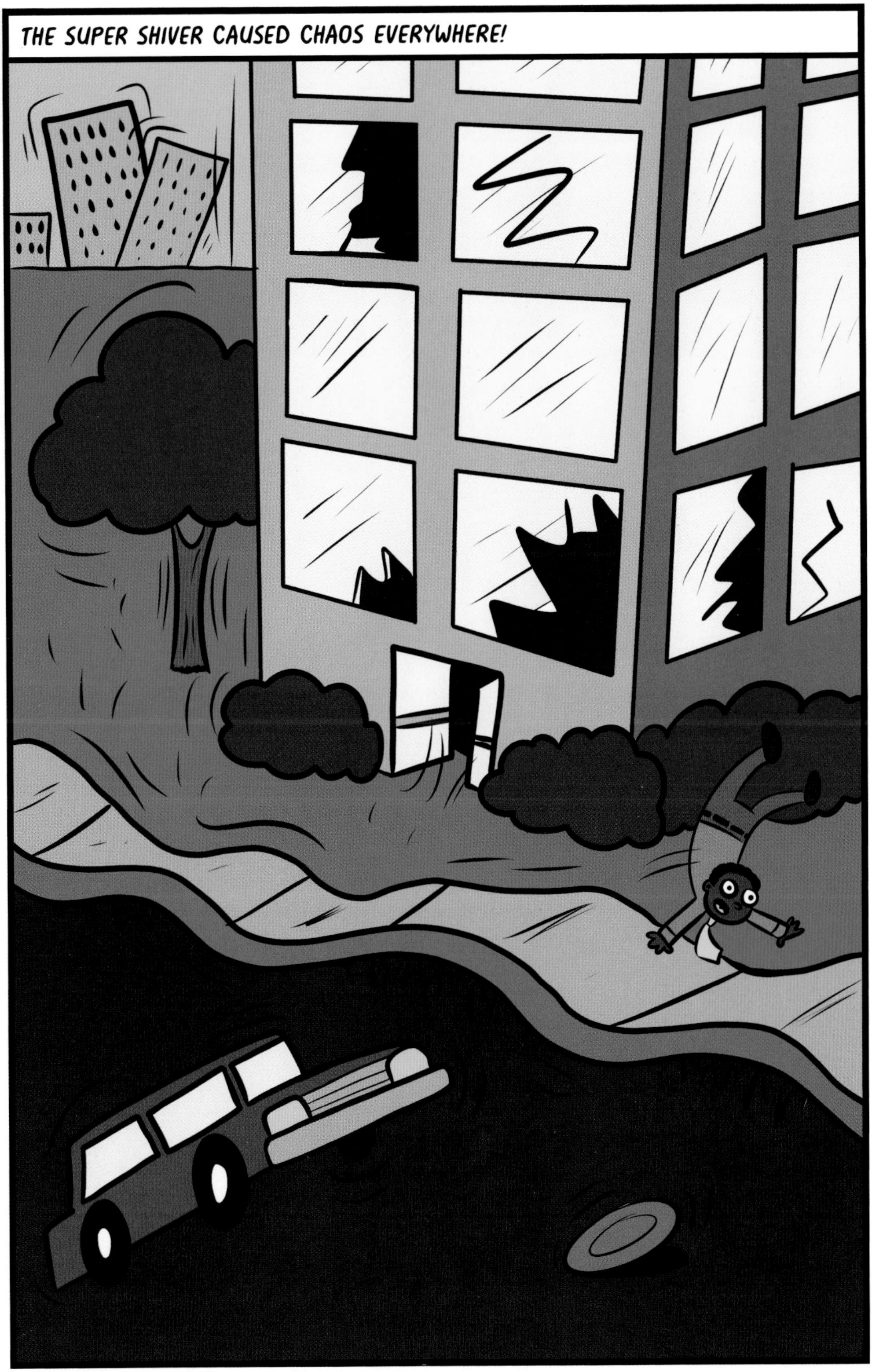
THE SUPER SHIVER CAUSED CHAOS EVERYWHERE!

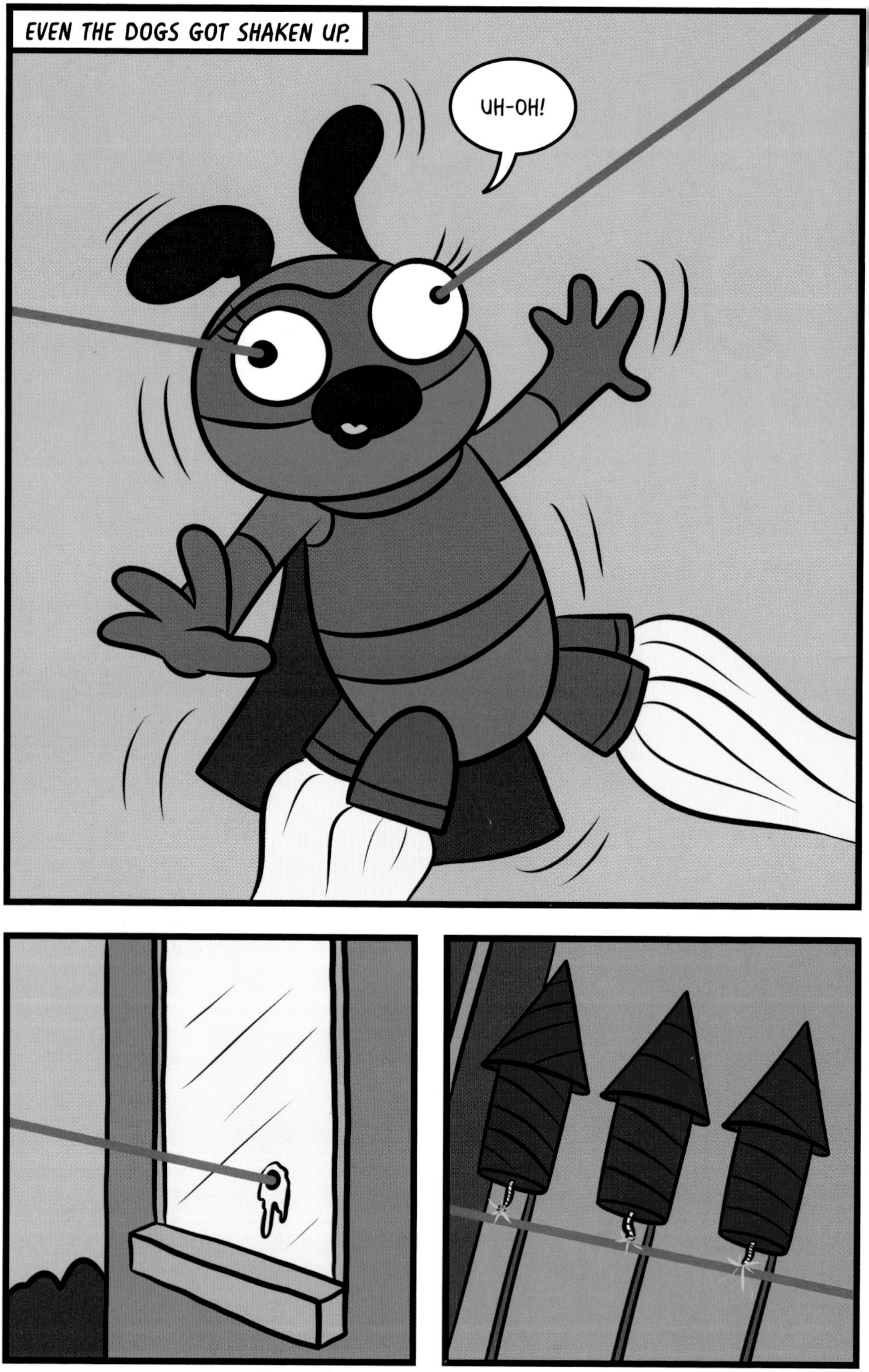
EVEN THE DOGS GOT SHAKEN UP.
UH-OH!

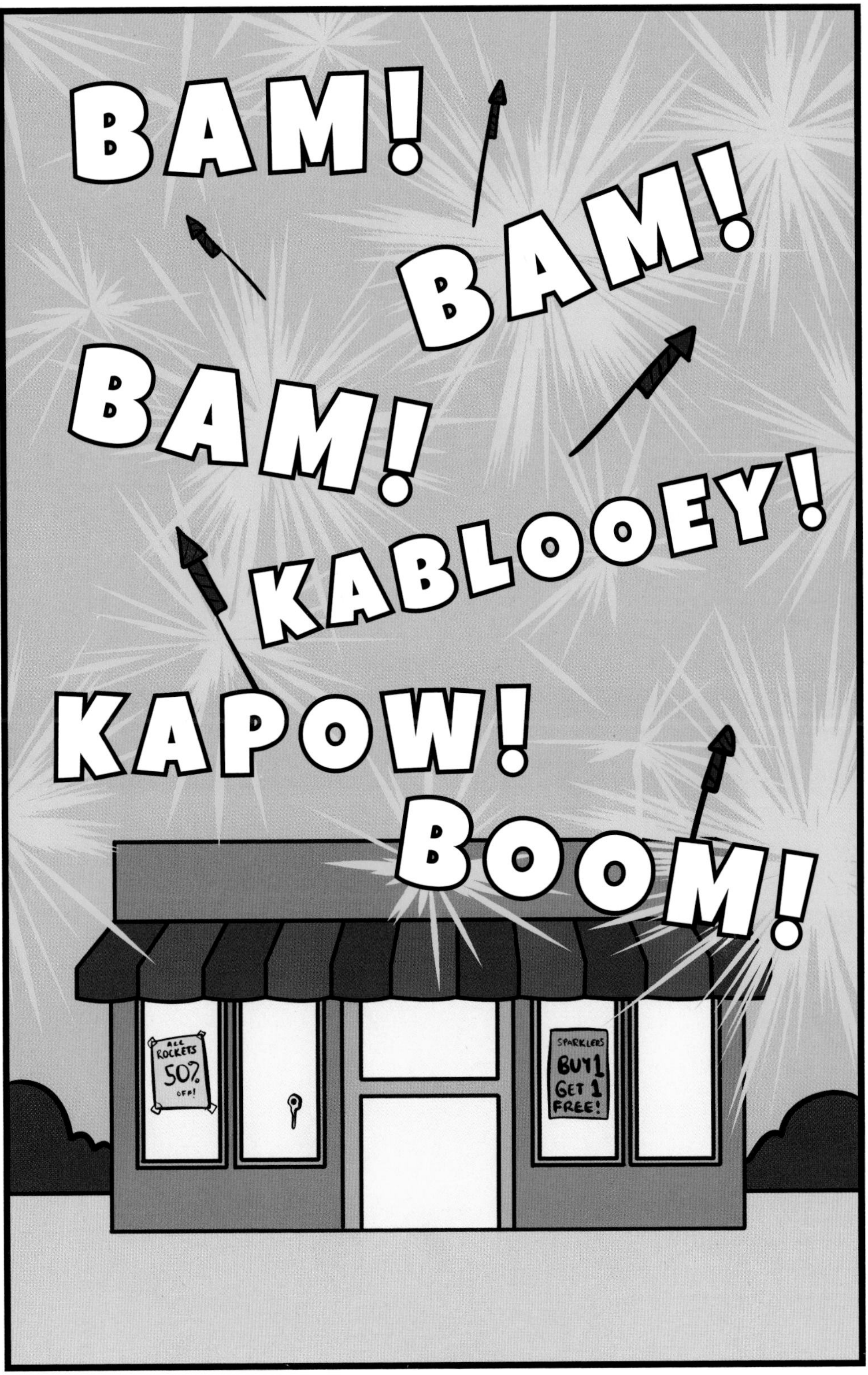
BAM!
BAM!
BAM!
KABLOOEY!
KAPOW!
BOOM!
ALL ROCKETS 50% OFF!
SPARKLERS BUY 1 GET 1 FREE!

59

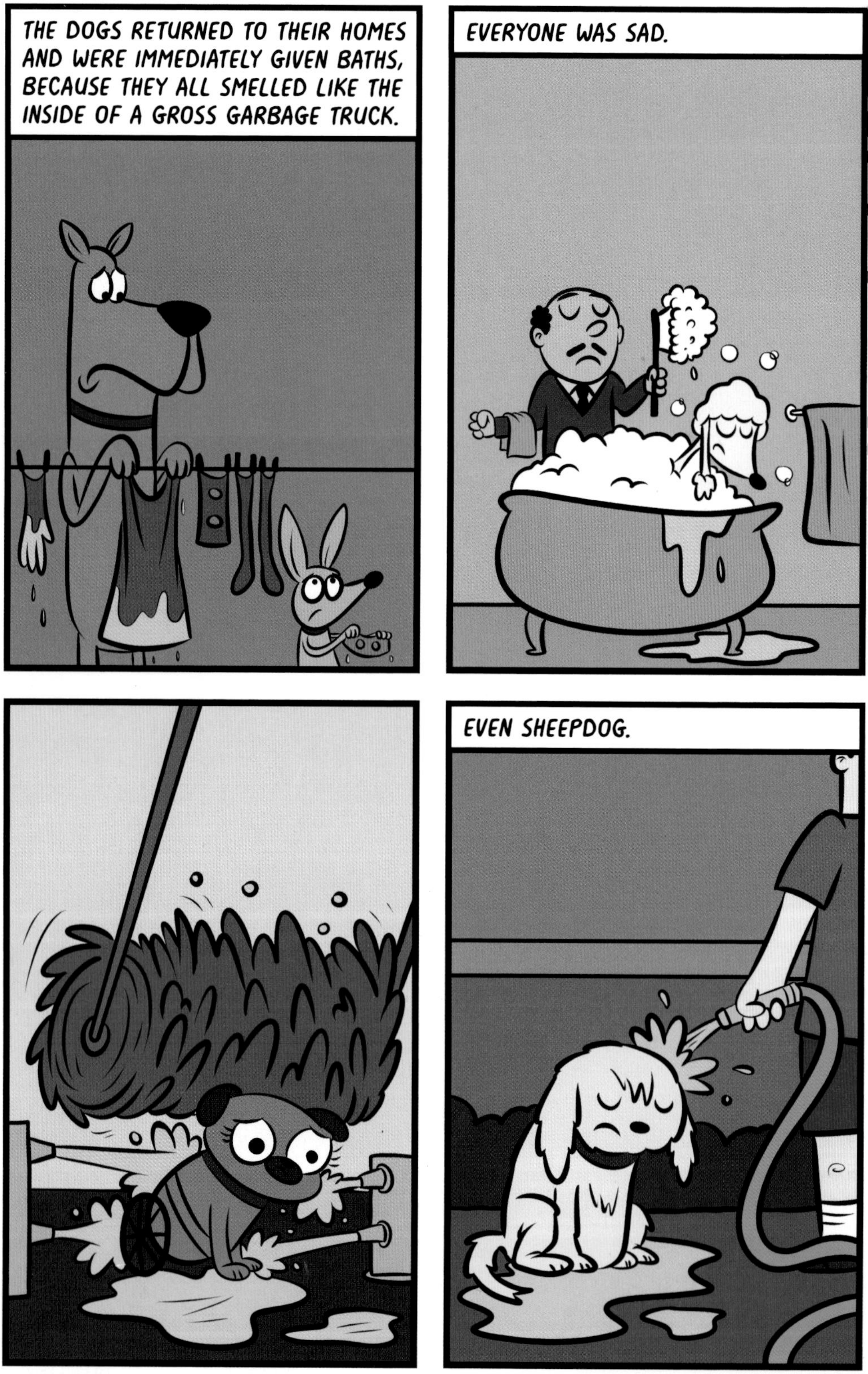
THE DOGS RETURNED TO THEIR HOMES AND WERE IMMEDIATELY GIVEN BATHS, BECAUSE THEY ALL SMELLED LIKE THE INSIDE OF A GROSS GARBAGE TRUCK.
EVERYONE WAS SAD.
EVEN SHEEPDOG.

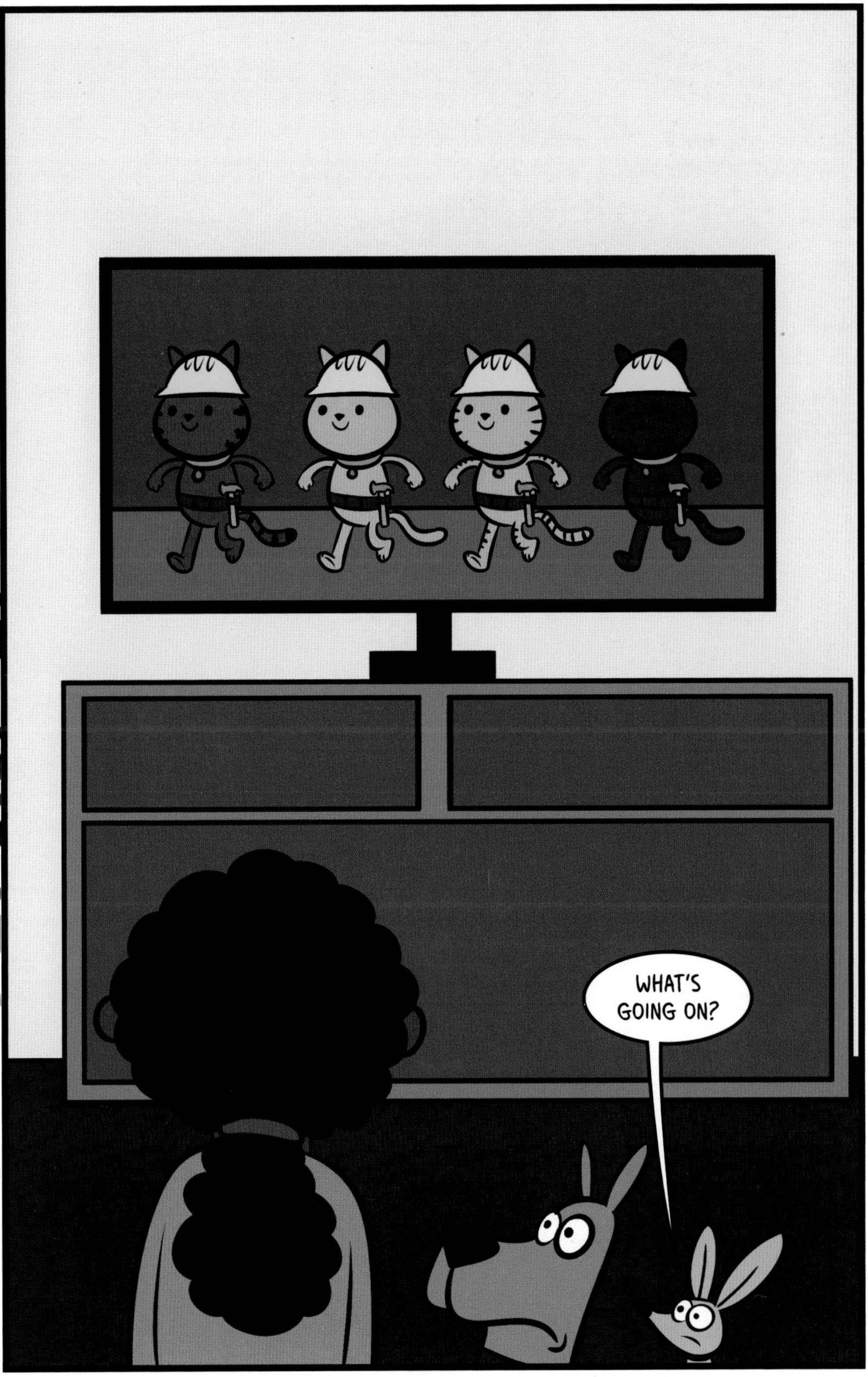
WHAT'S GOING ON?

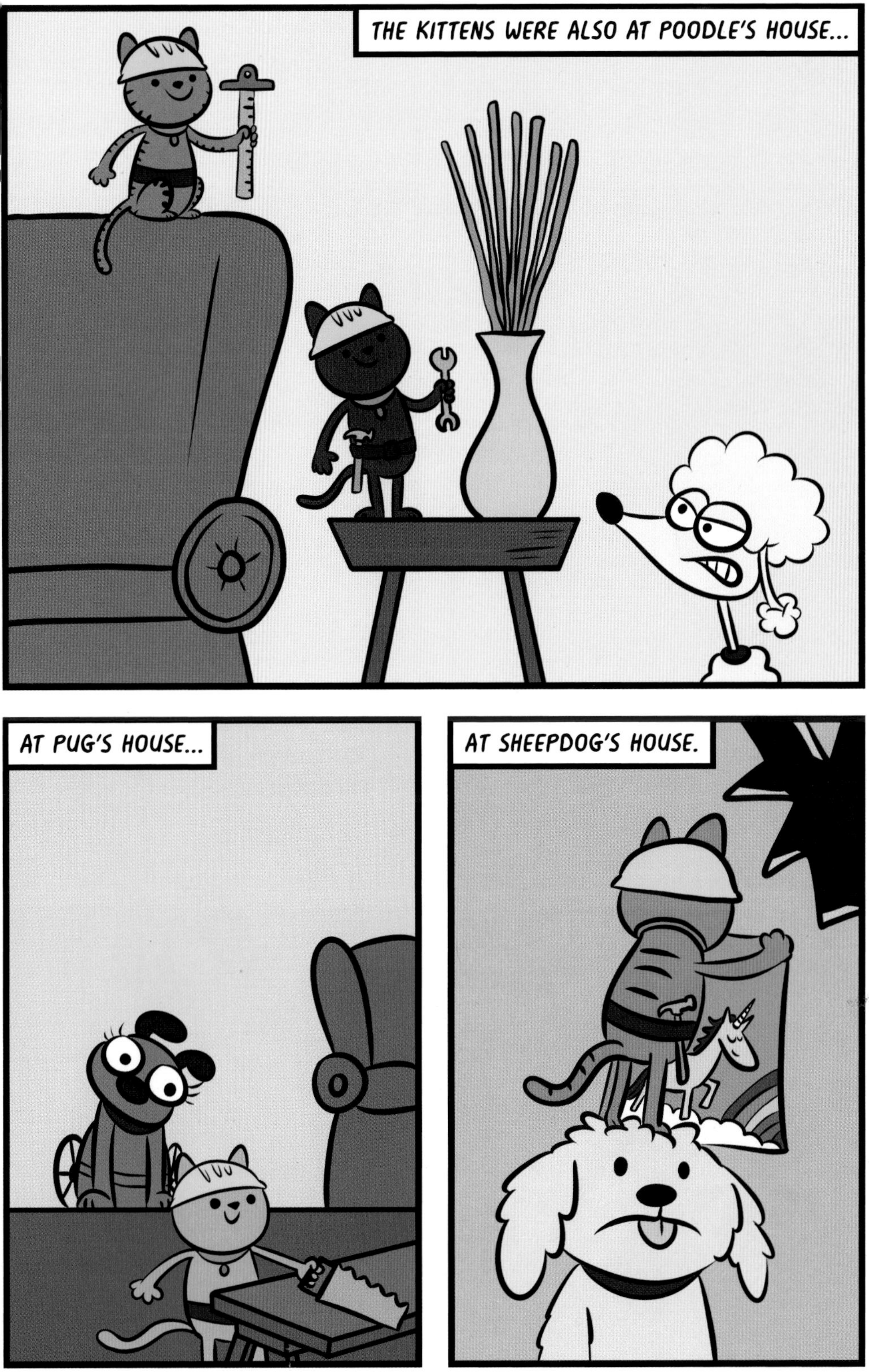
THE KITTENS WERE ALSO AT POODLE'S HOUSE...
AT PUG'S HOUSE...
AT SHEEPDOG'S HOUSE.

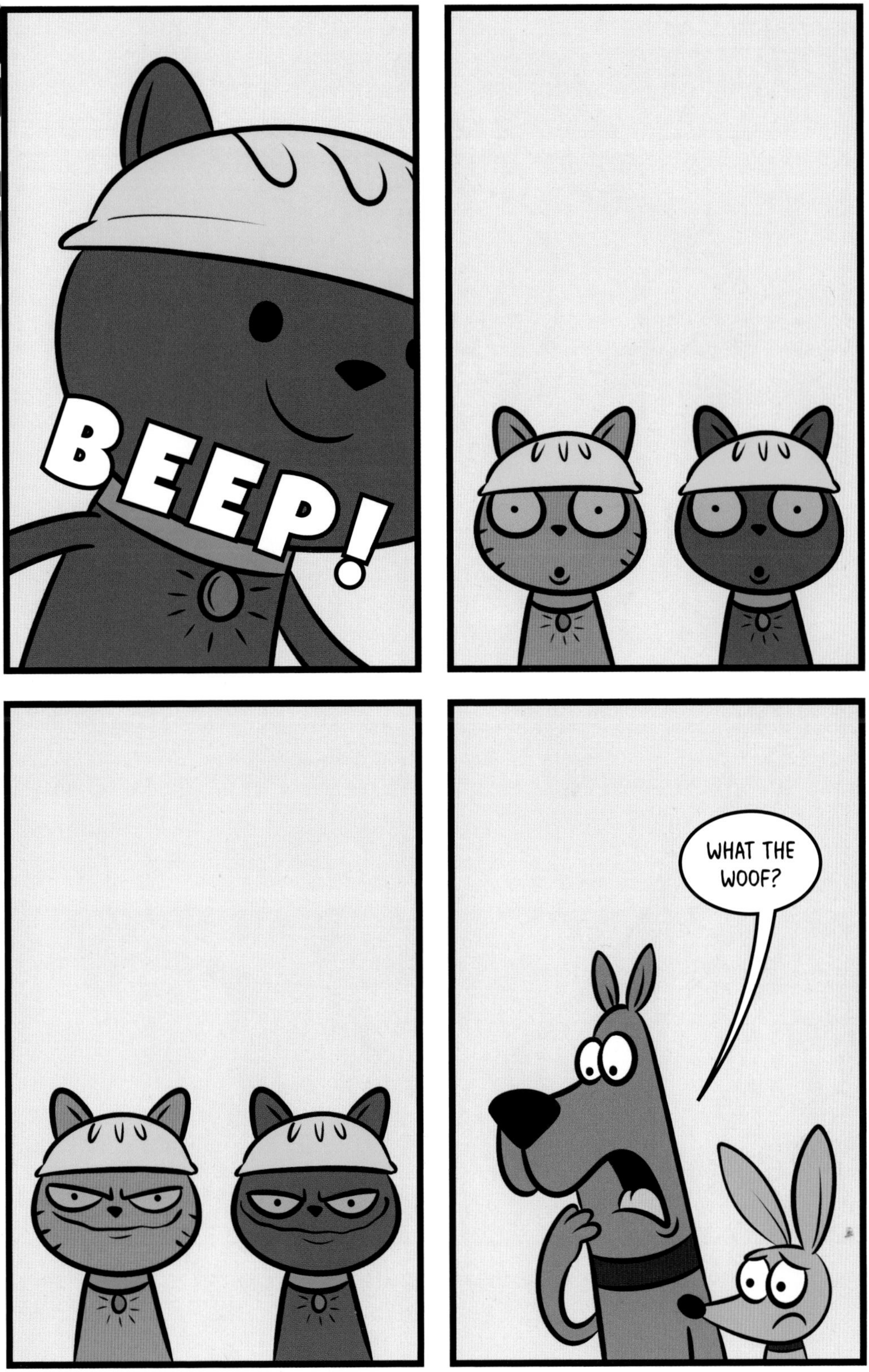
BEEP!
WHAT THE WOOF?

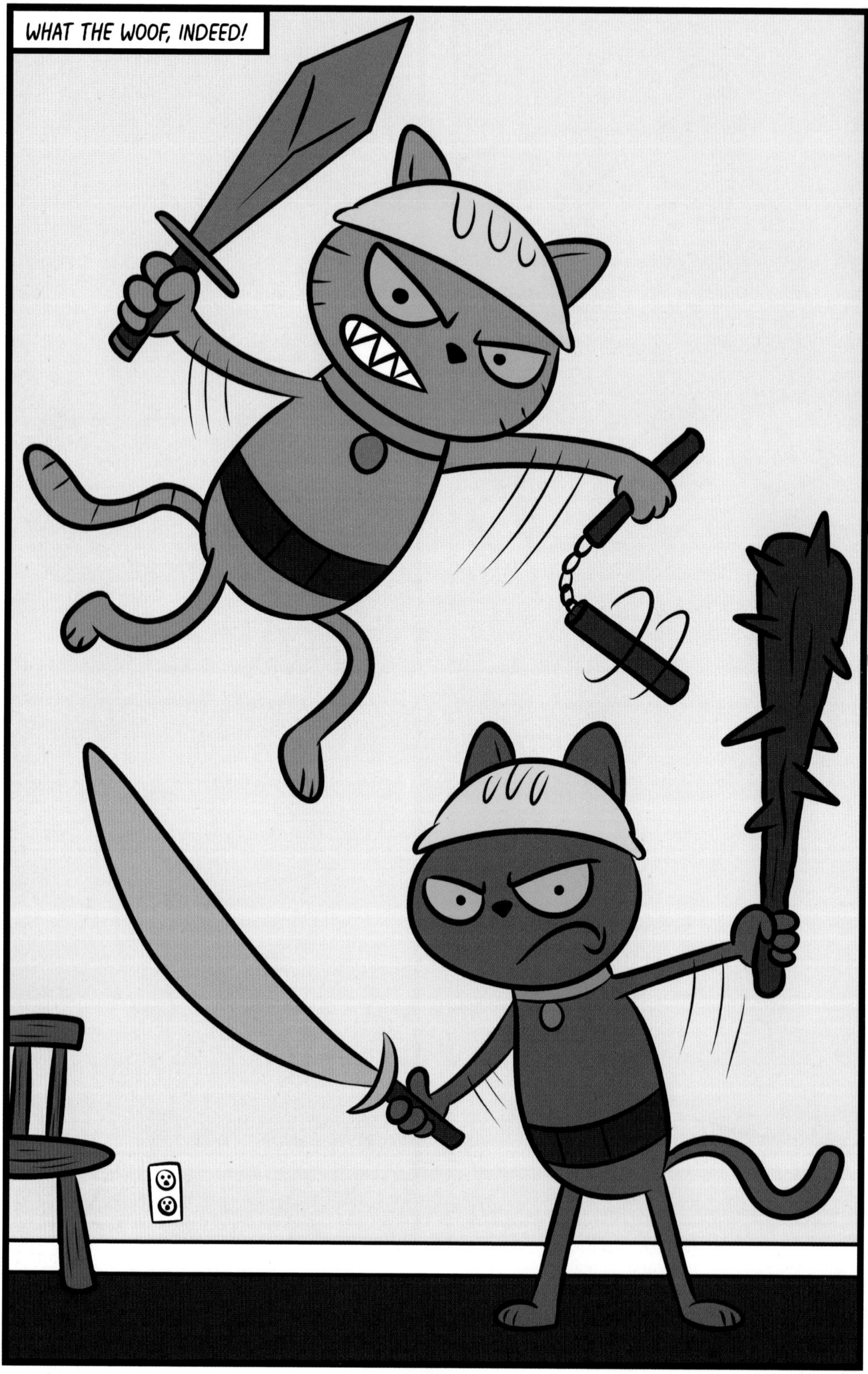
WHAT THE WOOF, INDEED!

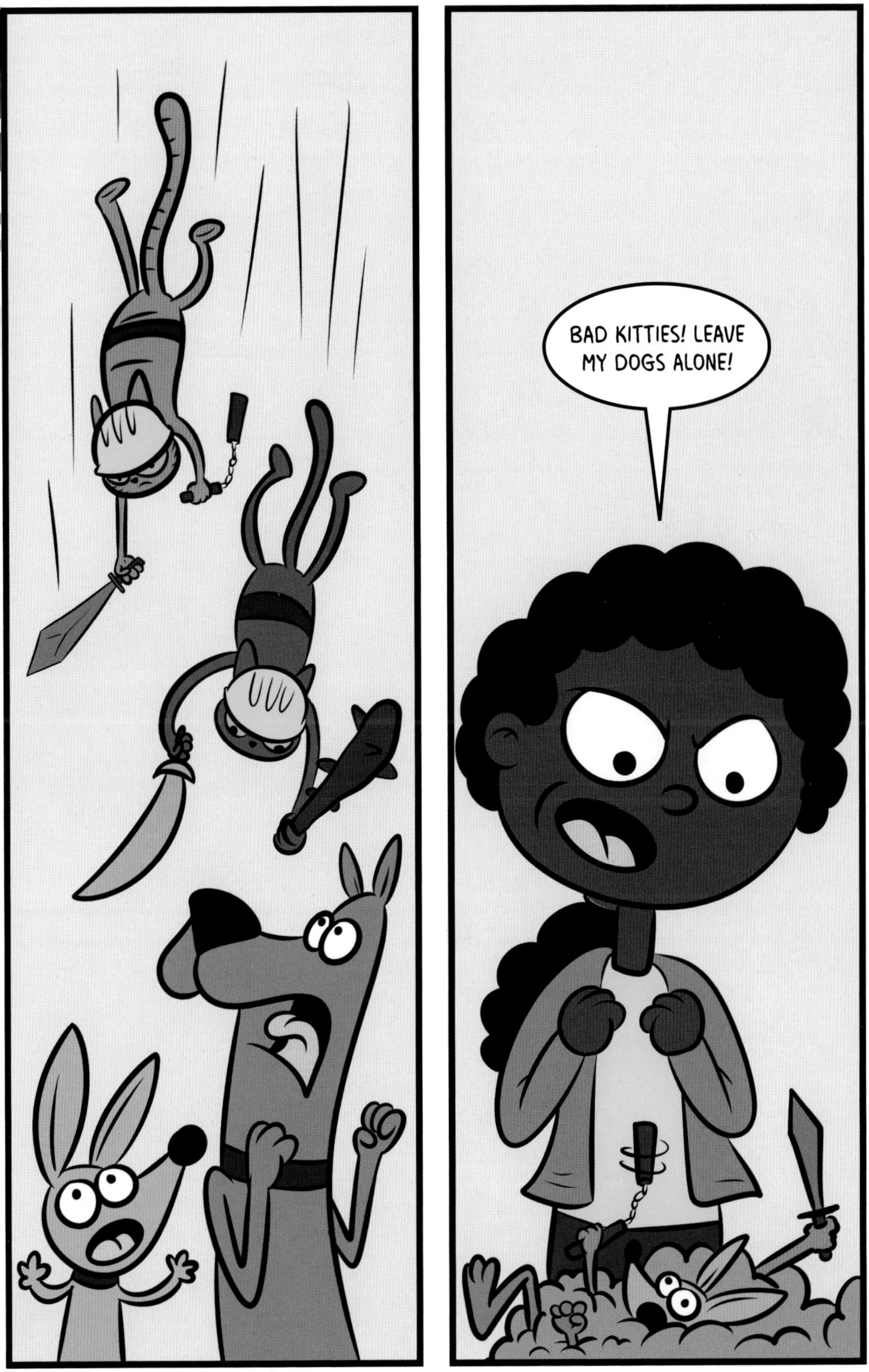
BAD KITTIES! LEAVE MY DOGS ALONE!

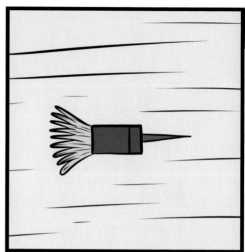

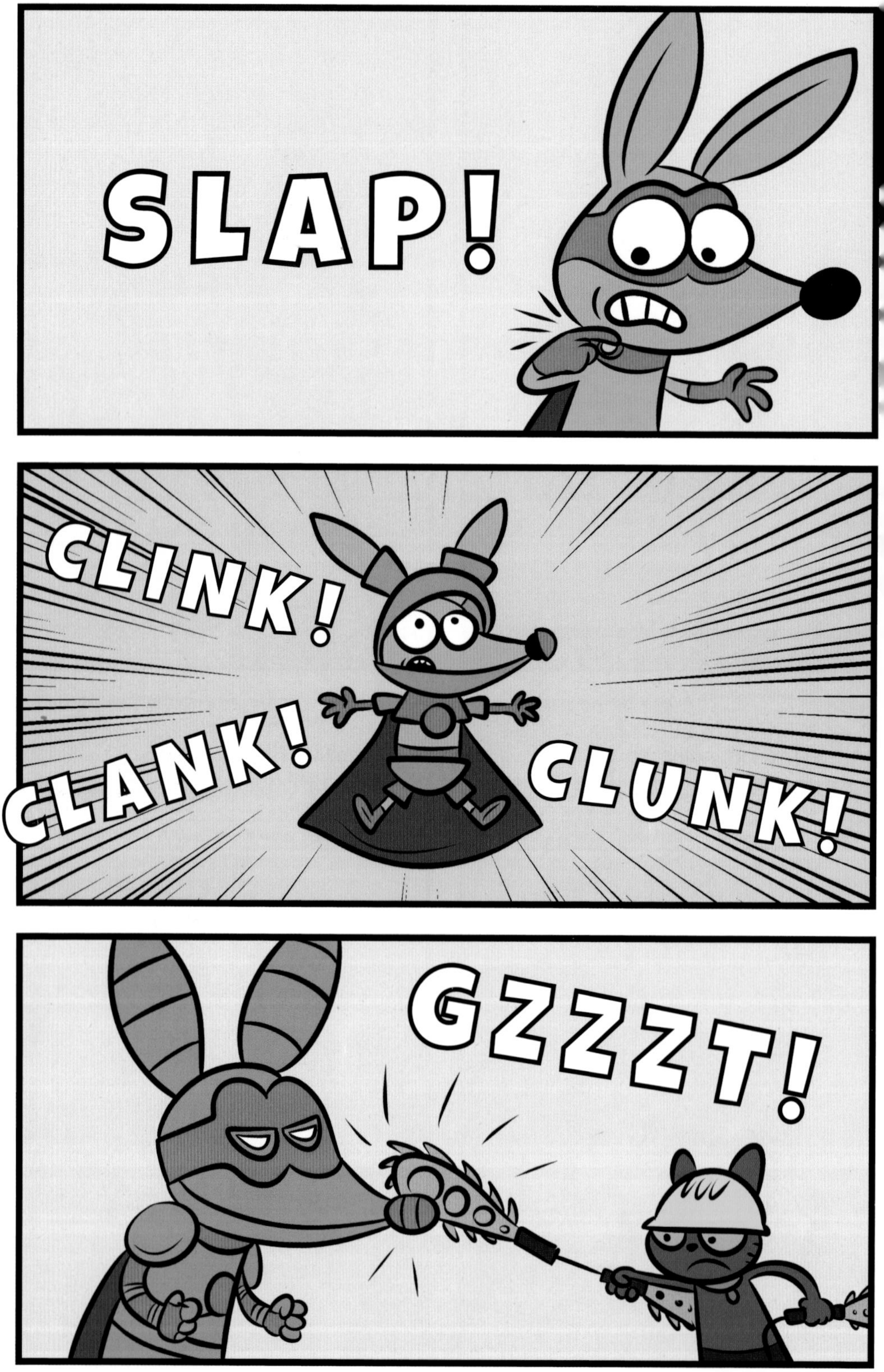
SLAP!
CLINK!
CLANK!
CLUNK!
GZZZT!

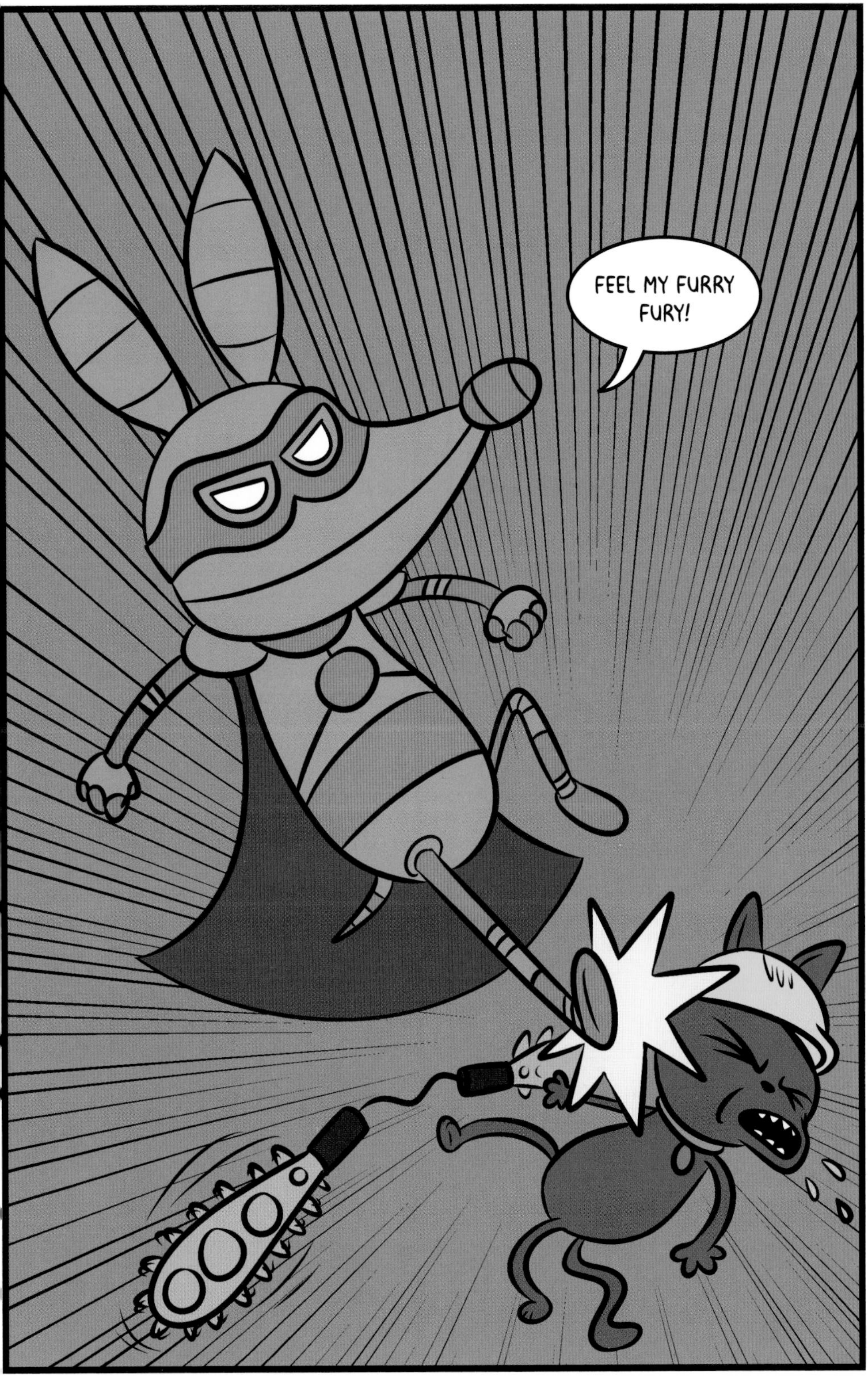
FEEL MY FURRY FURY!

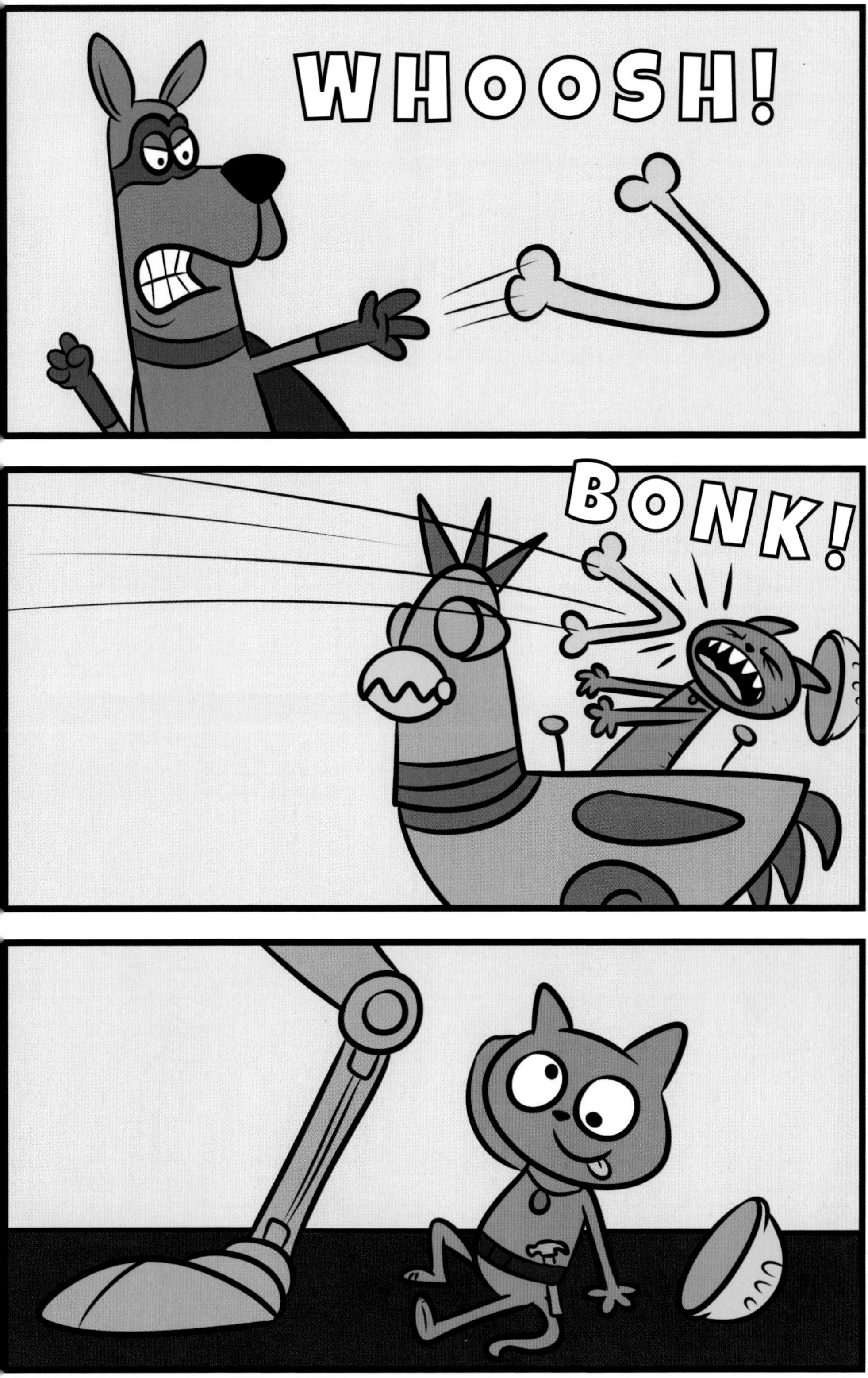
WHOOSH!
BONK!

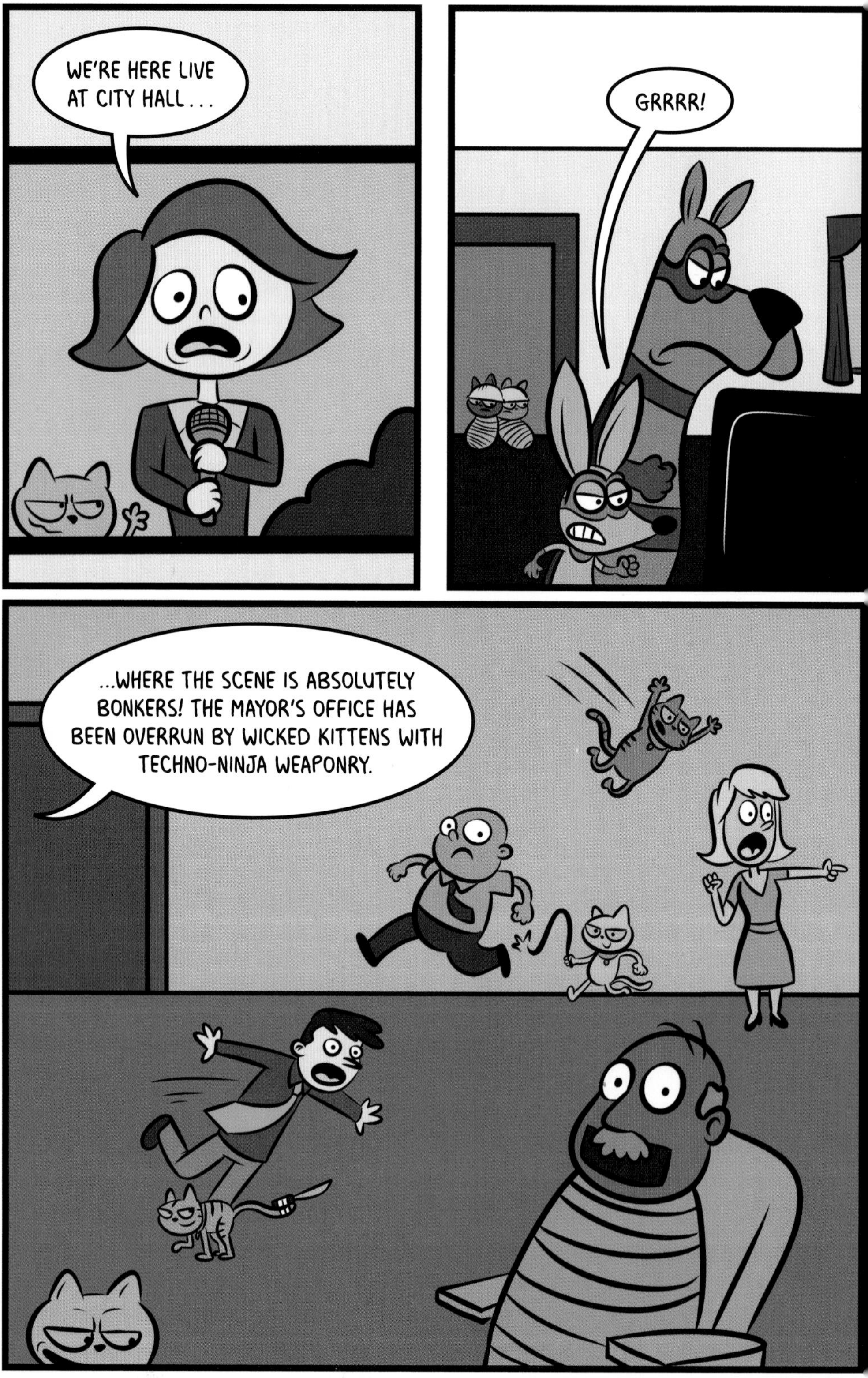
WE'RE HERE LIVE AT CITY HALL . . .
GRRRR!
...WHERE THE SCENE IS ABSOLUTELY BONKERS! THE MAYOR'S OFFICE HAS BEEN OVERRUN BY WICKED KITTENS WITH TECHNO-NINJA WEAPONRY.

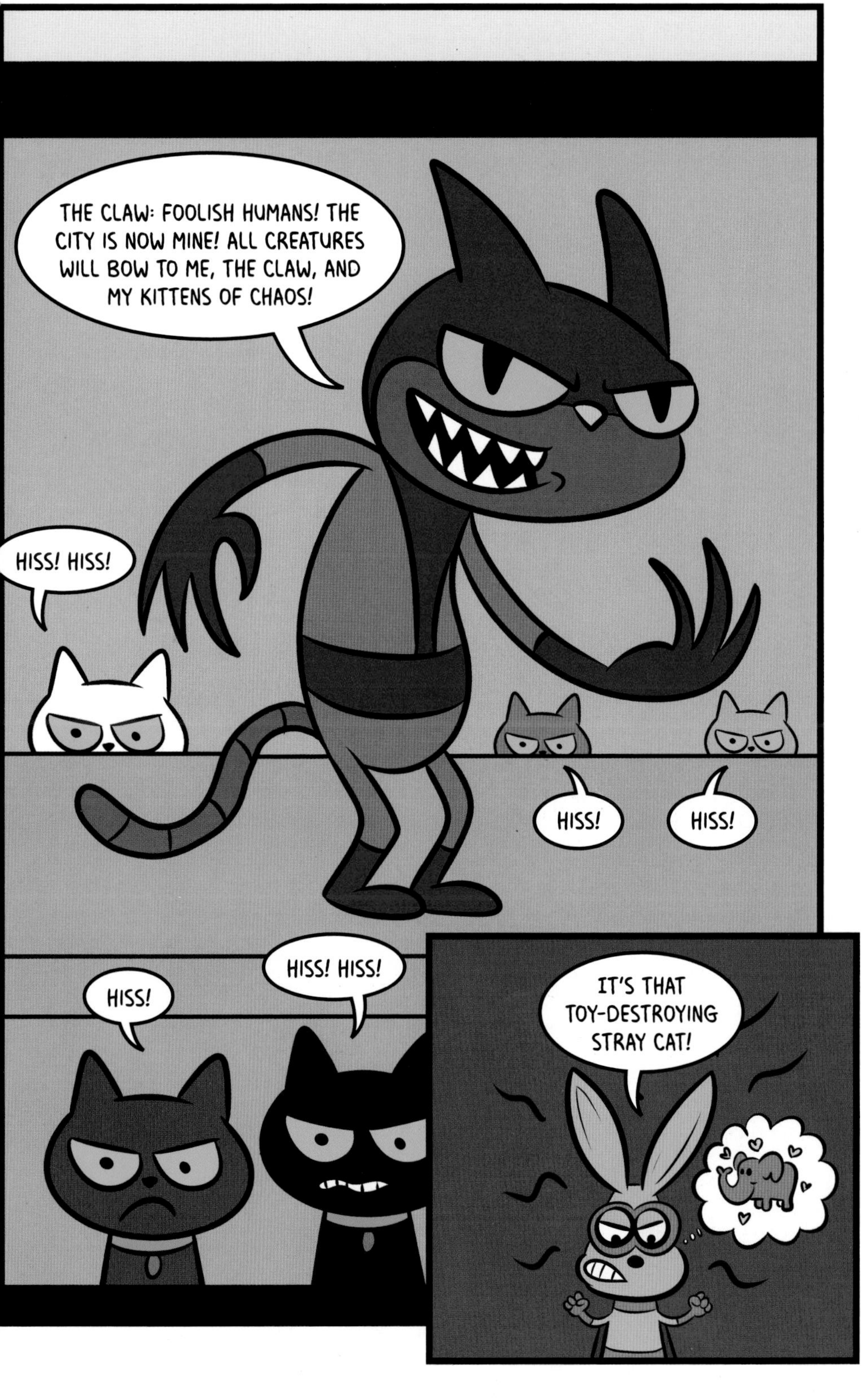
THE CLAW: FOOLISH HUMANS! THE CITY IS NOW MINE! ALL CREATURES WILL BOW TO ME, THE CLAW, AND MY KITTENS OF CHAOS!
HISS! HISS!
HISS!
HISS!
HISS!
HISS! HISS!
IT'S THAT TOY-DESTROYING STRAY CAT!

81

LET'S TRY THAT HATCH!

I CAN'T GET IT OPEN.

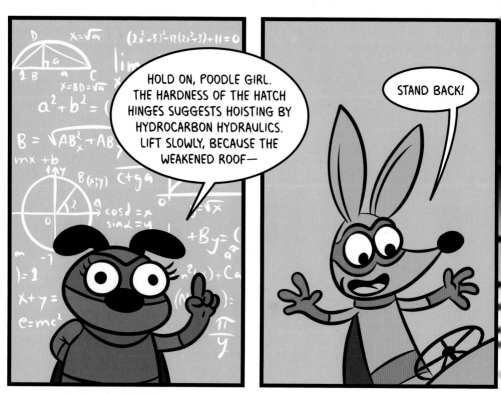

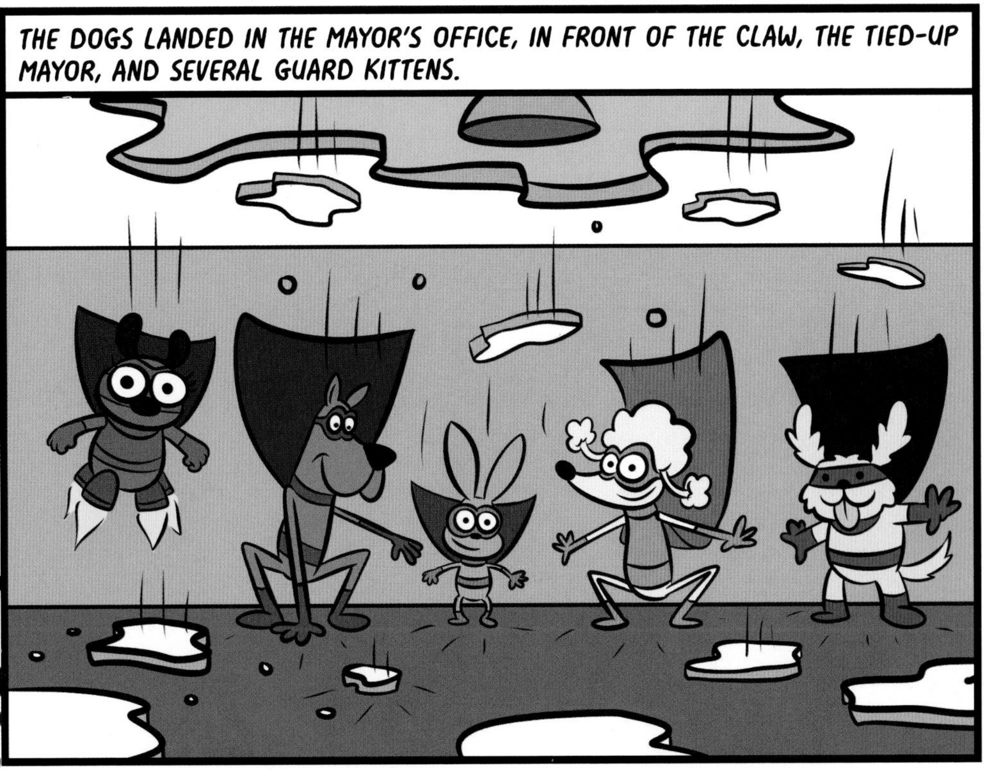
THE DOGS LANDED IN THE MAYOR'S OFFICE, IN FRONT OF THE CLAW, THE TIED-UP MAYOR, AND SEVERAL GUARD KITTENS.

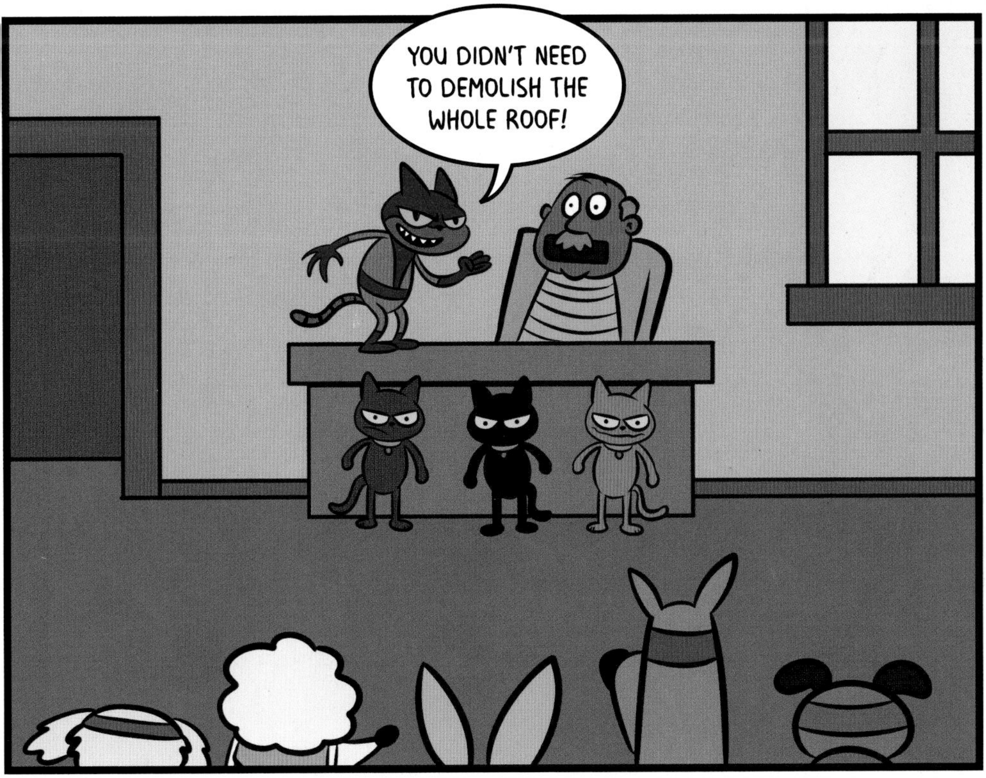
YOU DIDN'T NEED TO DEMOLISH THE WHOLE ROOF!

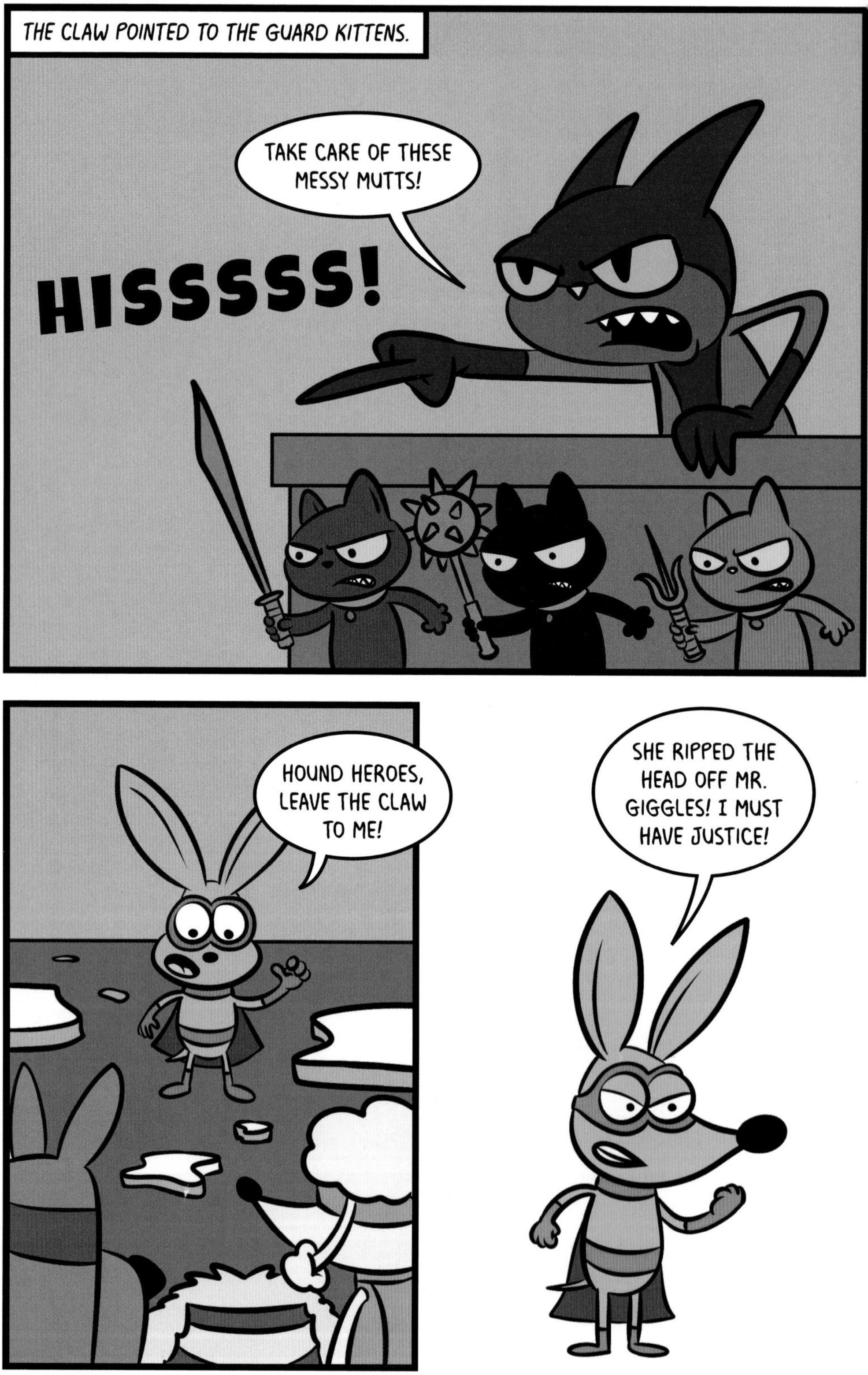
THE CLAW POINTED TO THE GUARD KITTENS.
TAKE CARE OF THESE MESSY MUTTS!
HISSSSS!
HOUND HEROES, LEAVE THE CLAW TO ME!
SHE RIPPED THE HEAD OFF MR. GIGGLES! I MUST HAVE JUSTICE!

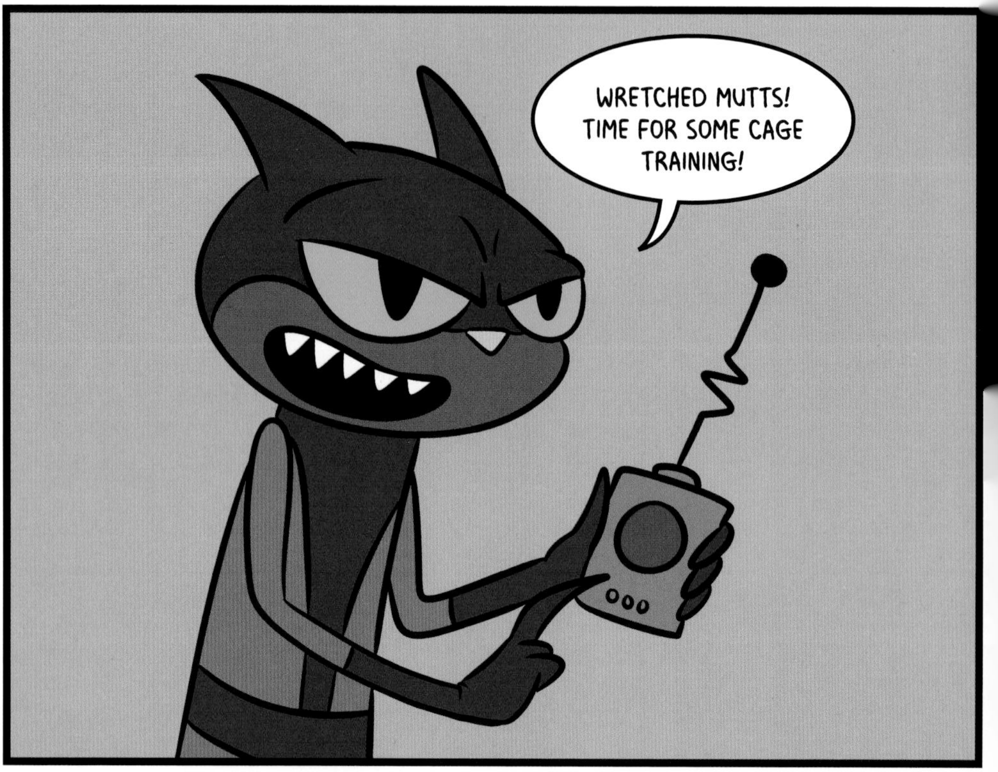
WRETCHED MUTTS! TIME FOR SOME CAGE TRAINING!

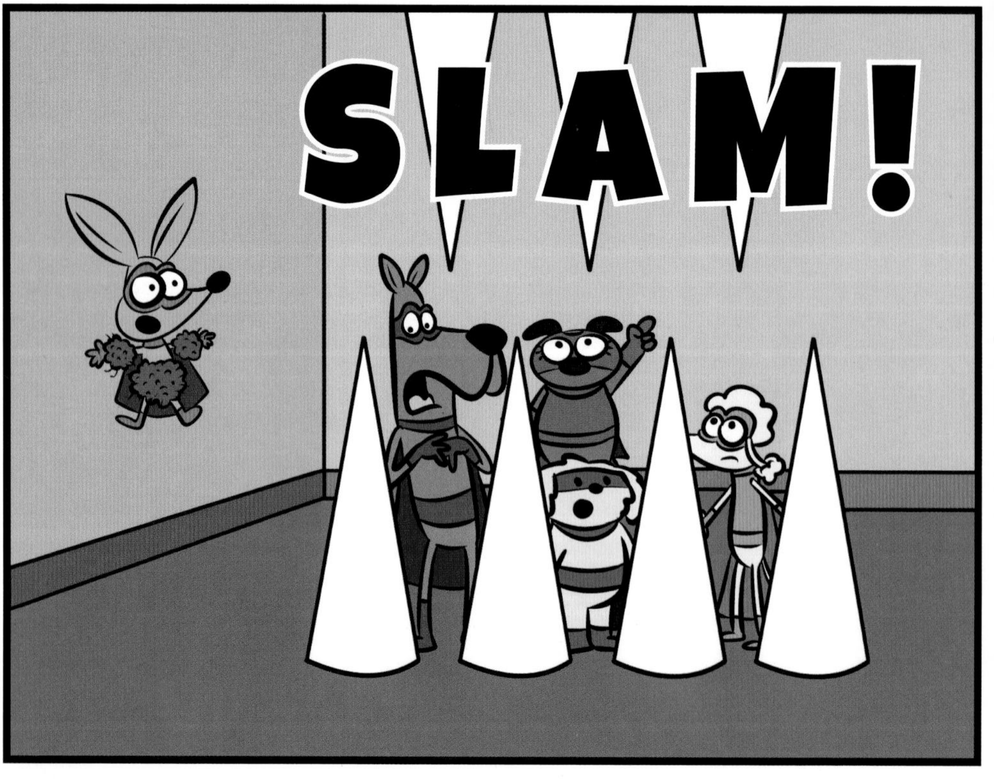
SLAM!

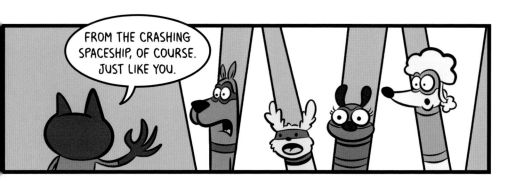

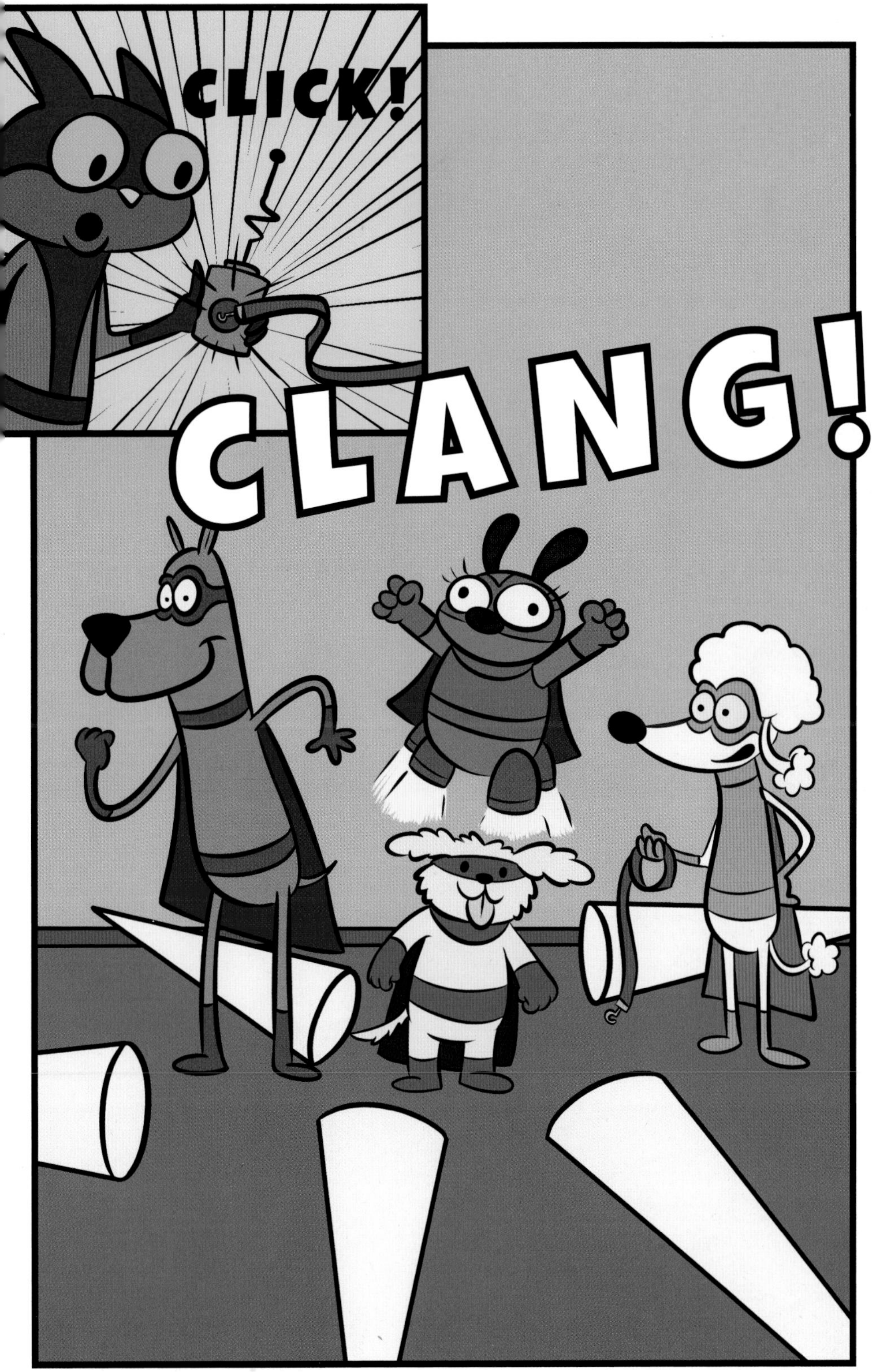
CLICK!
CLANG!

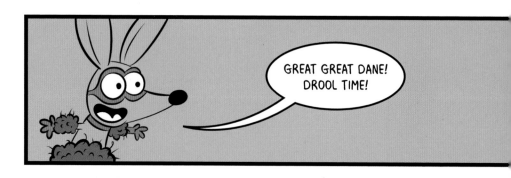

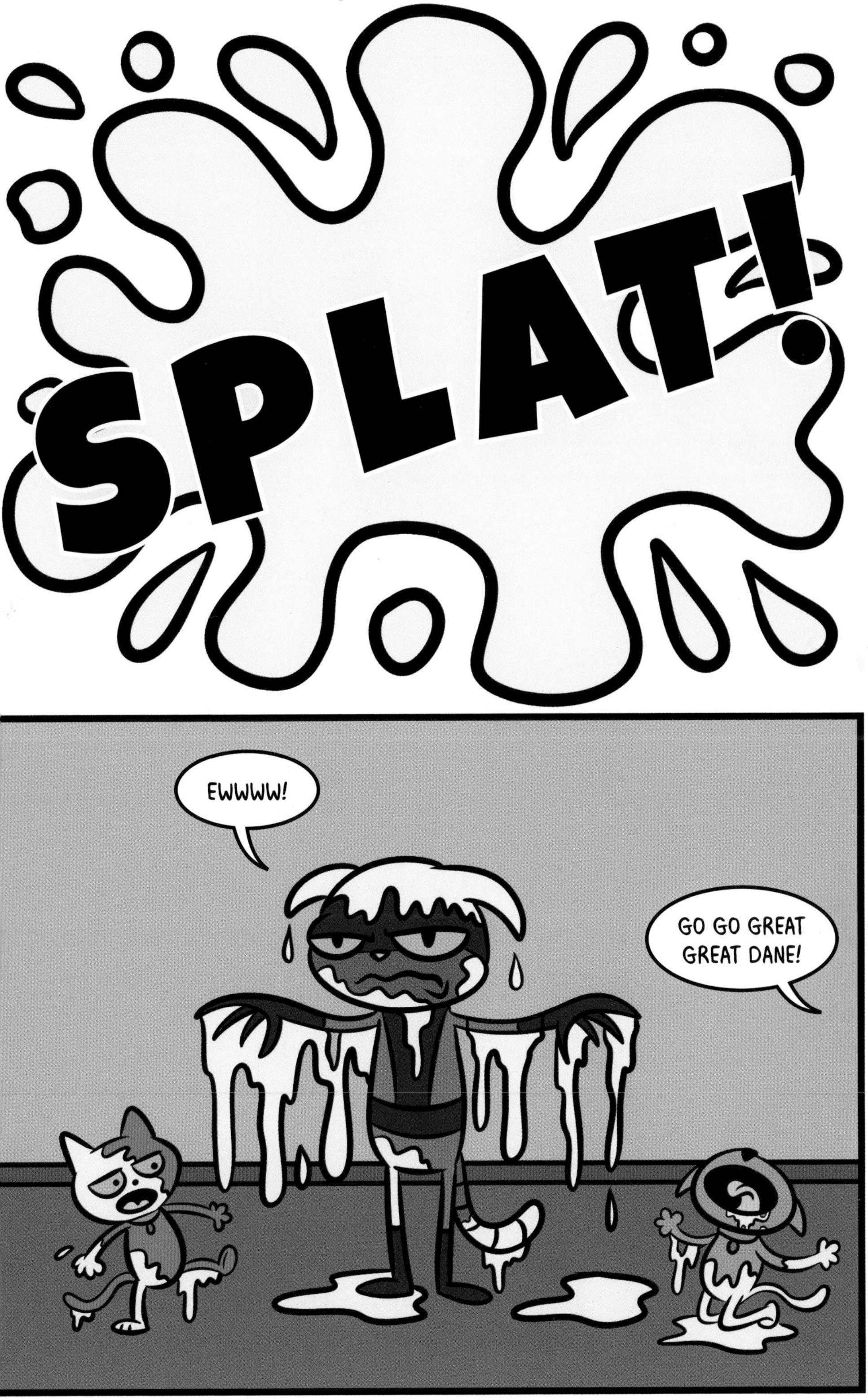
SPLAT!
EWWWW!
GO GO GREAT GREAT DANE!

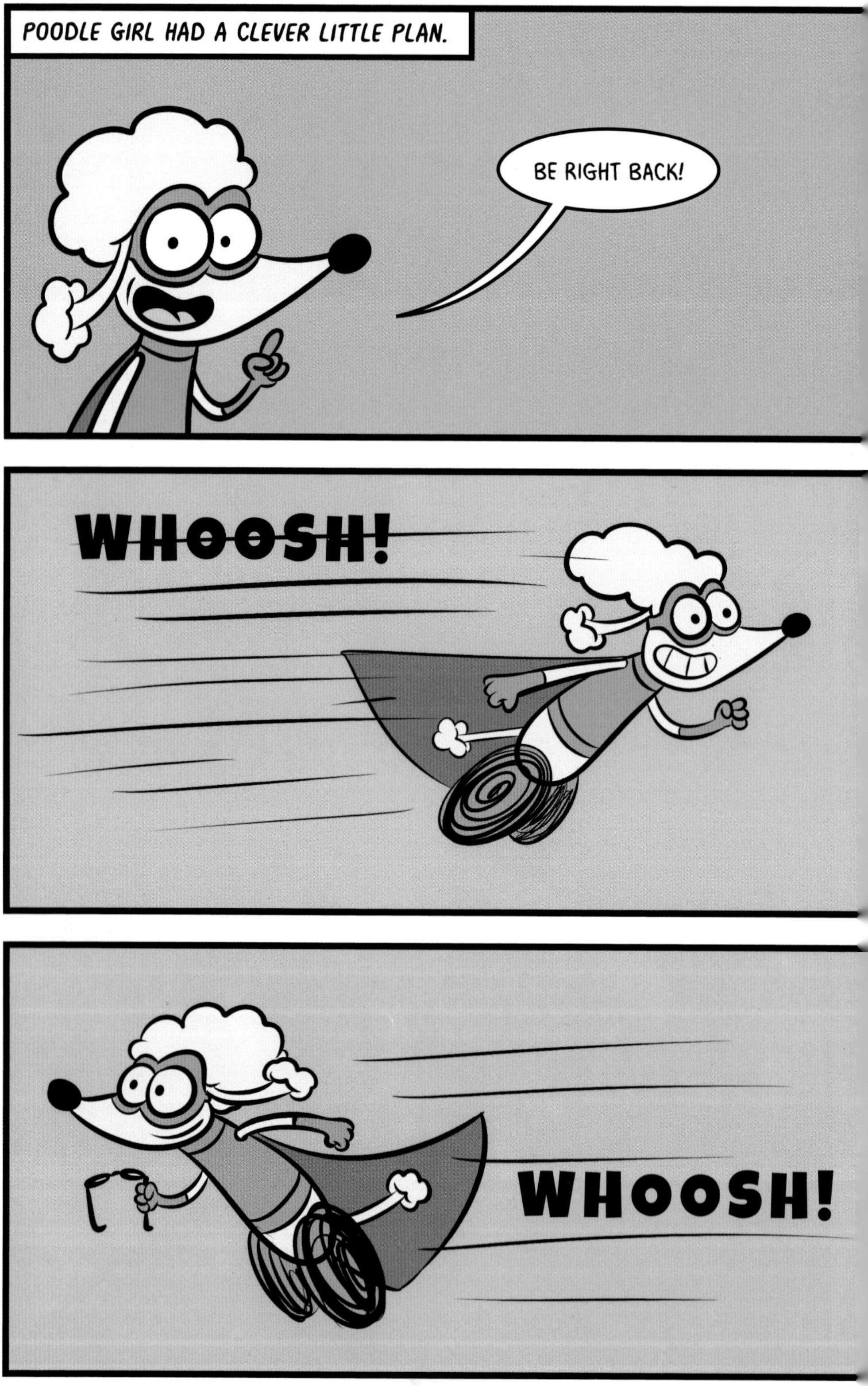
POODLE GIRL HAD A CLEVER LITTLE PLAN.
BE RIGHT BACK!
WHOOSH!
WHOOSH!

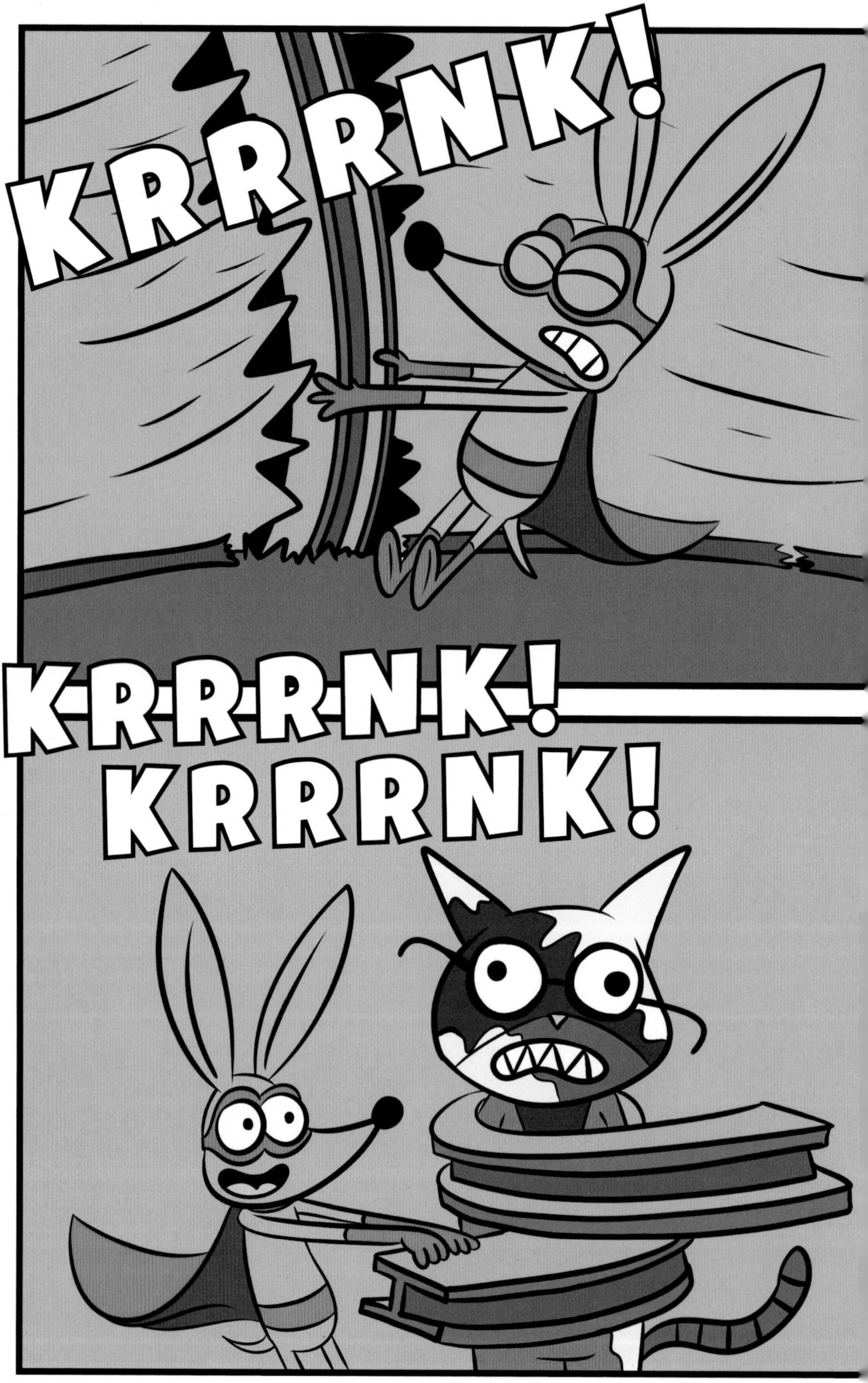
KRRRNK!
KRRRNK!
KRRRNK!

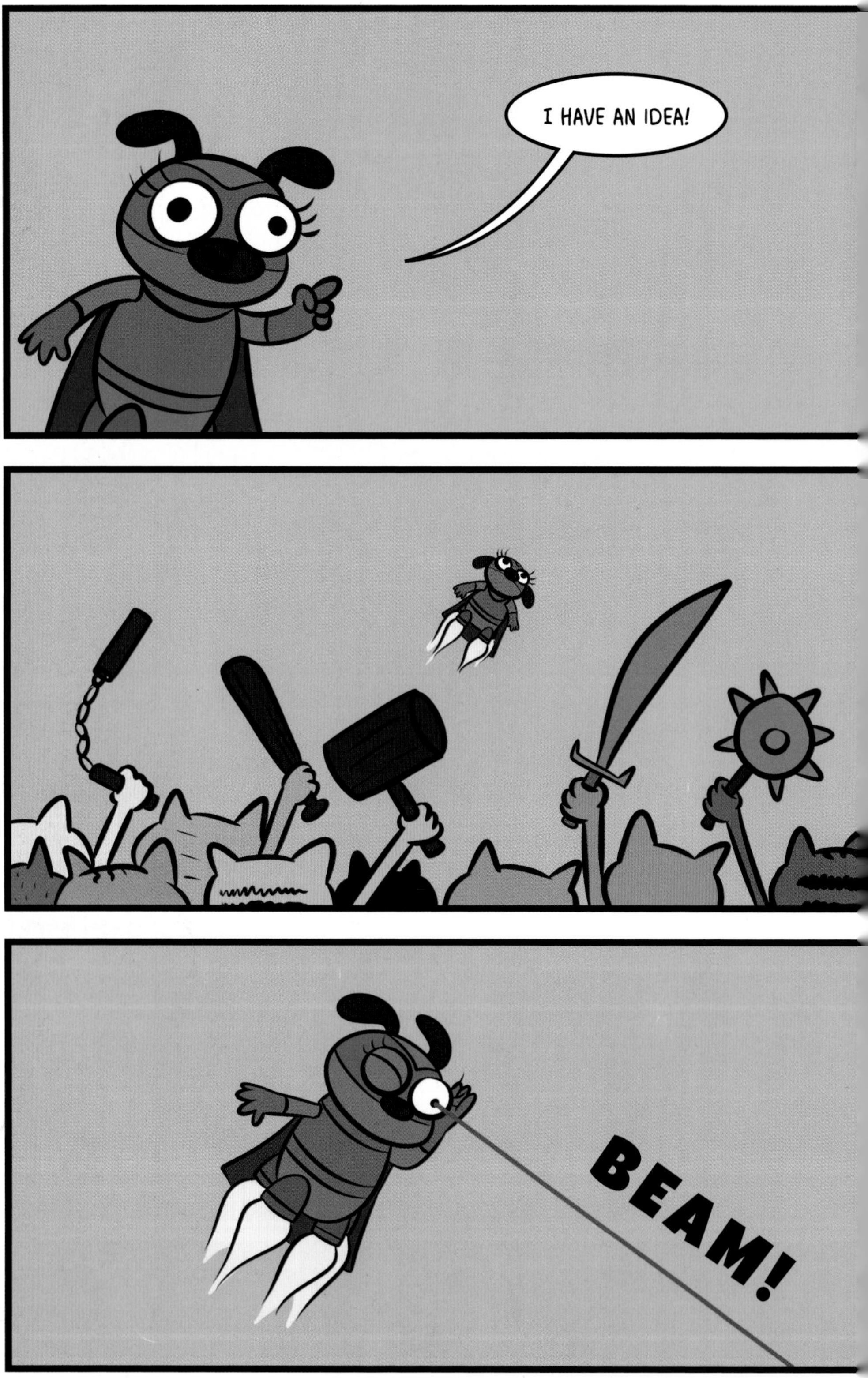
I HAVE AN IDEA!
BEAM!

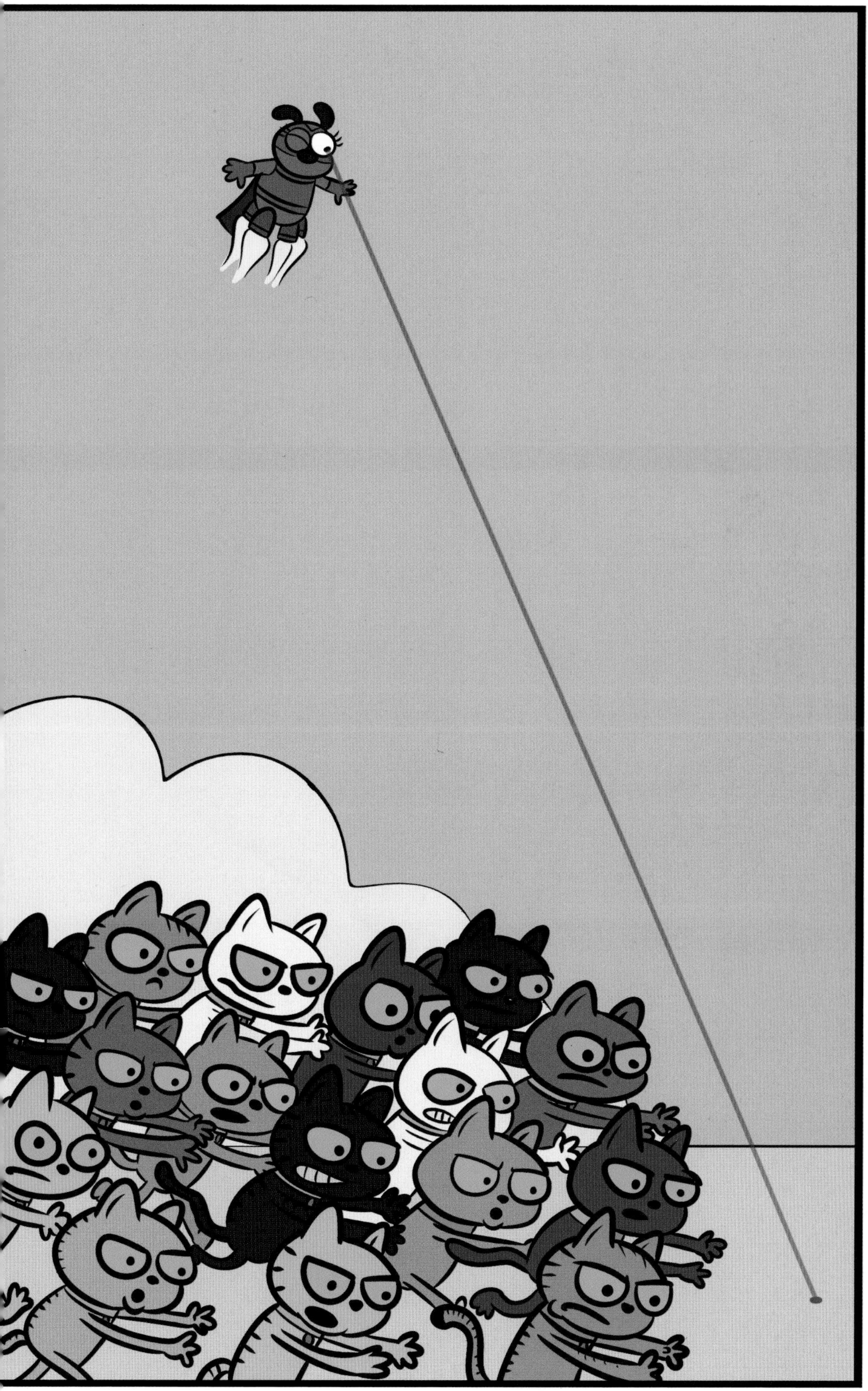

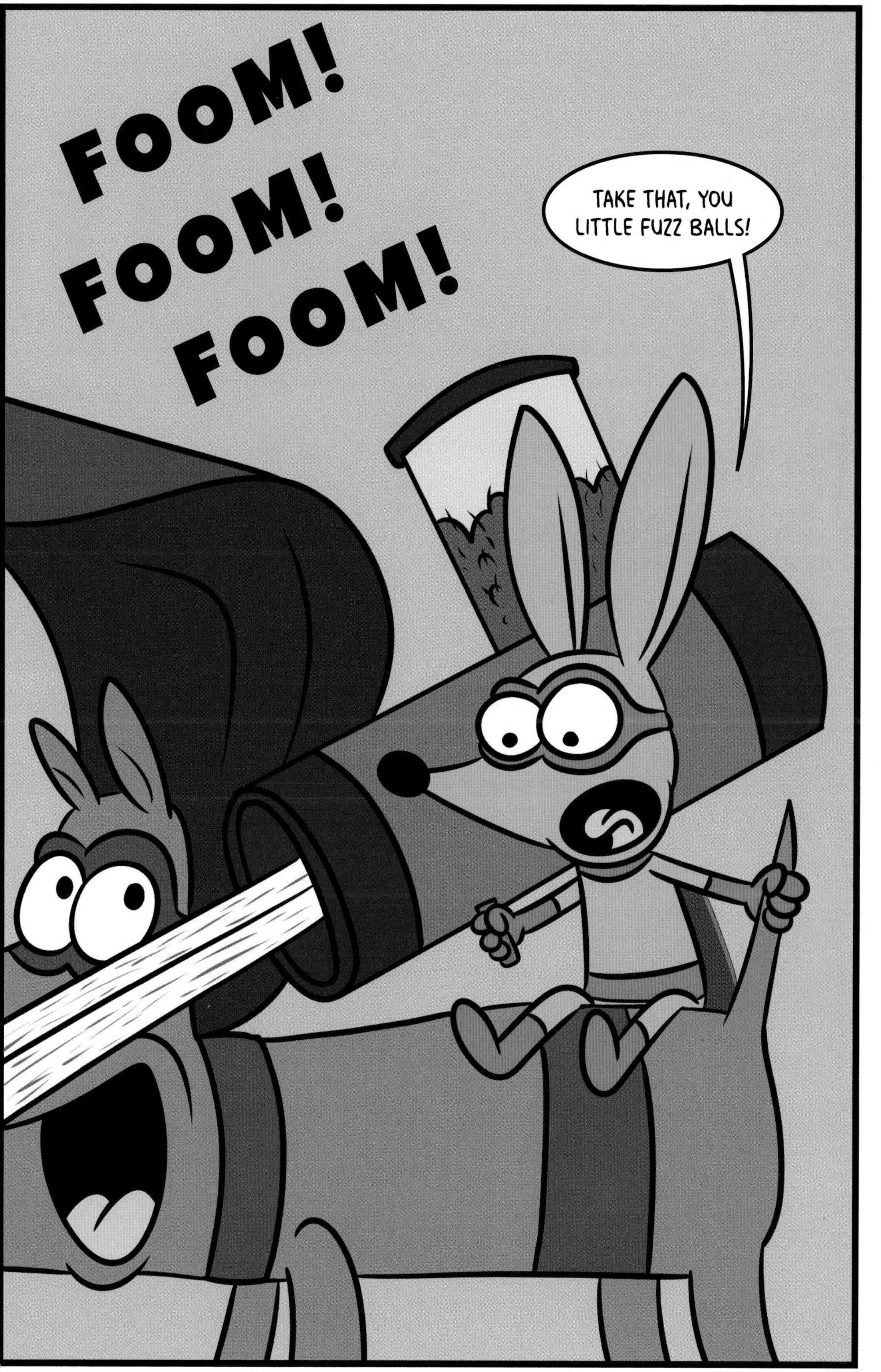
FOOM!
FOOM!
FOOM!
TAKE THAT, YOU LITTLE FUZZ BALLS!

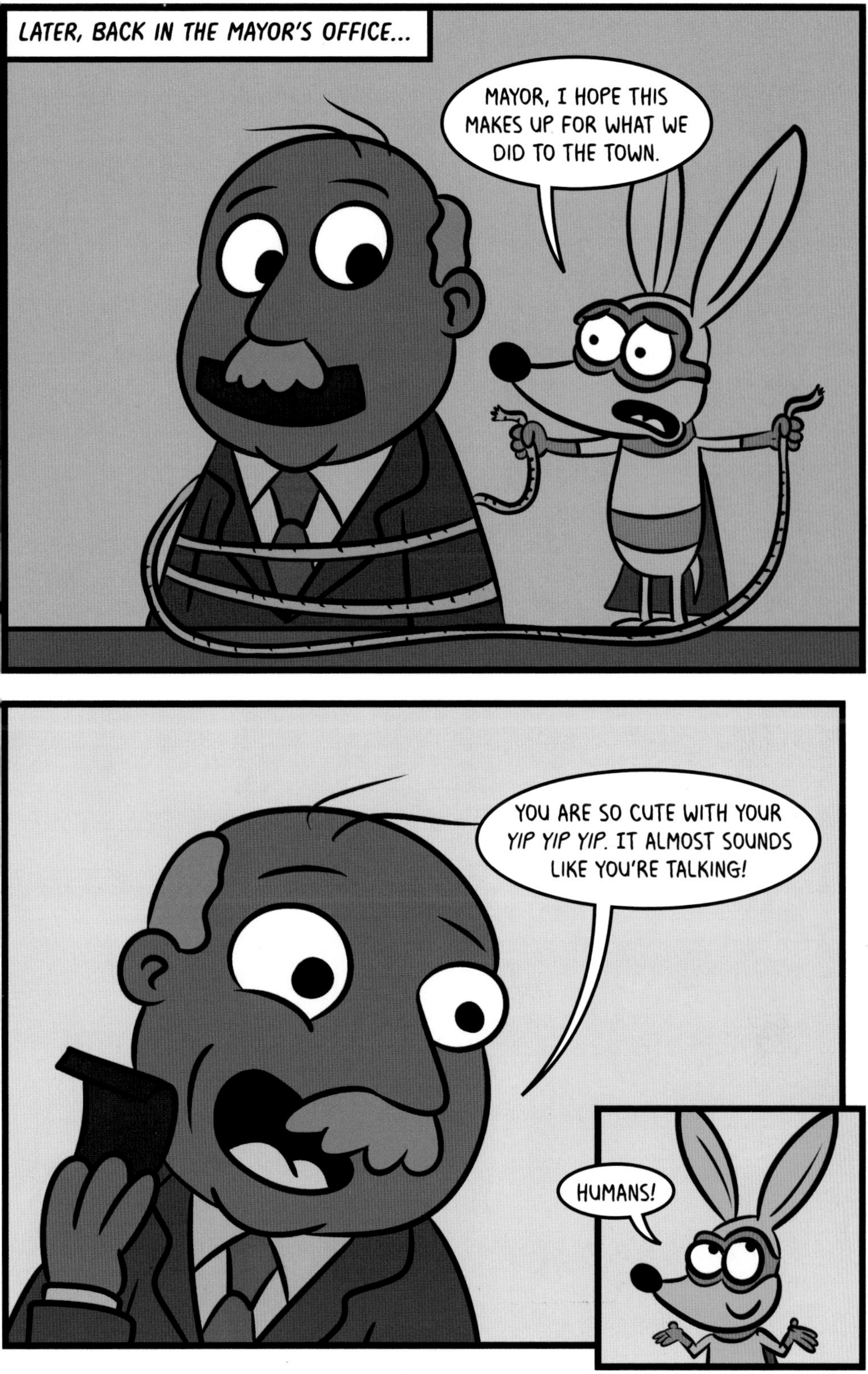
LATER, BACK IN THE MAYOR'S OFFICE...
MAYOR, I HOPE THIS MAKES UP FOR WHAT WE DID TO THE TOWN.
YOU ARE SO CUTE WITH YOUR *YIP YIP YIP*. IT ALMOST SOUNDS LIKE YOU'RE TALKING!
HUMANS!

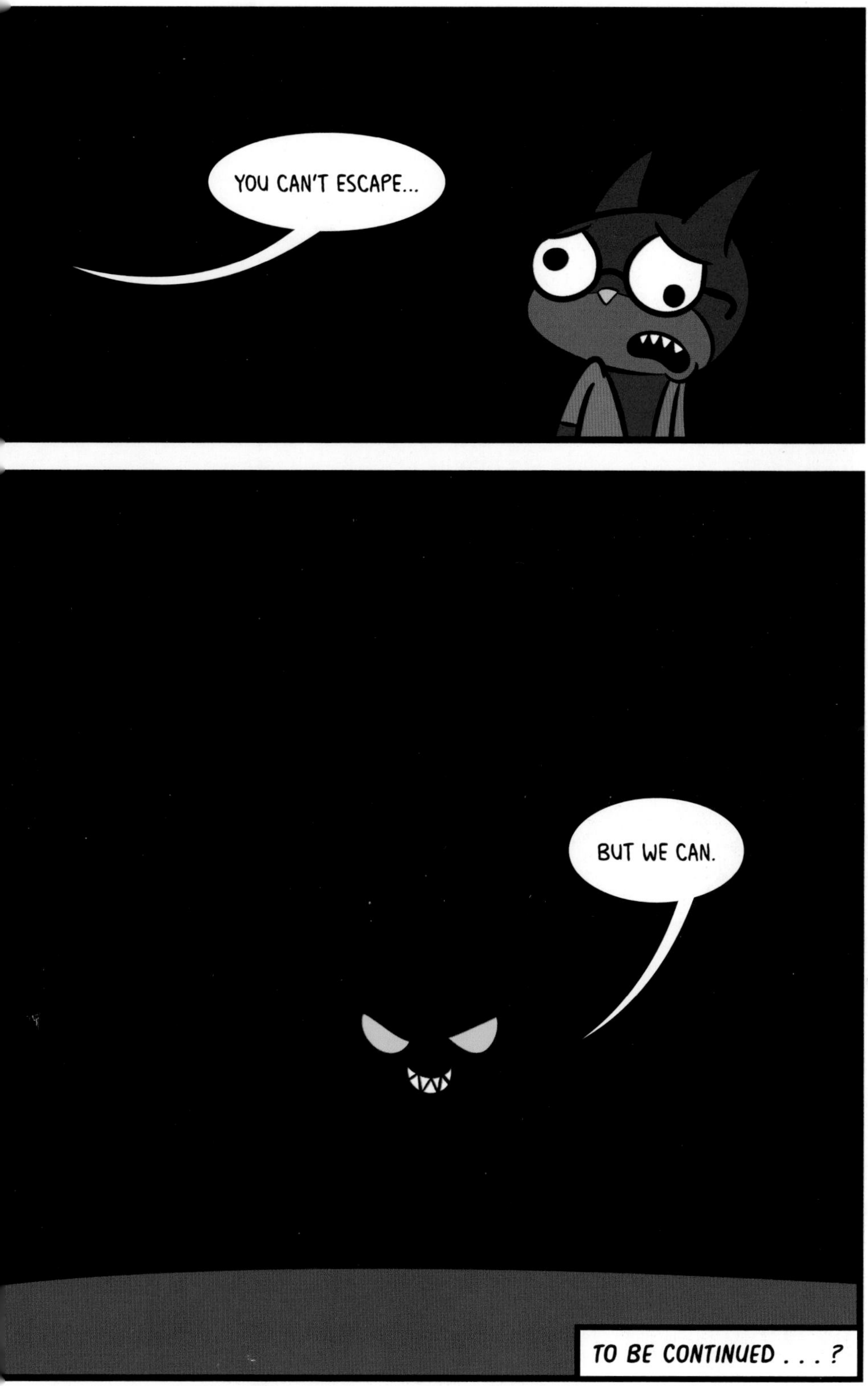
YOU CAN'T ESCAPE...
BUT WE CAN.
TO BE CONTINUED . . . ?

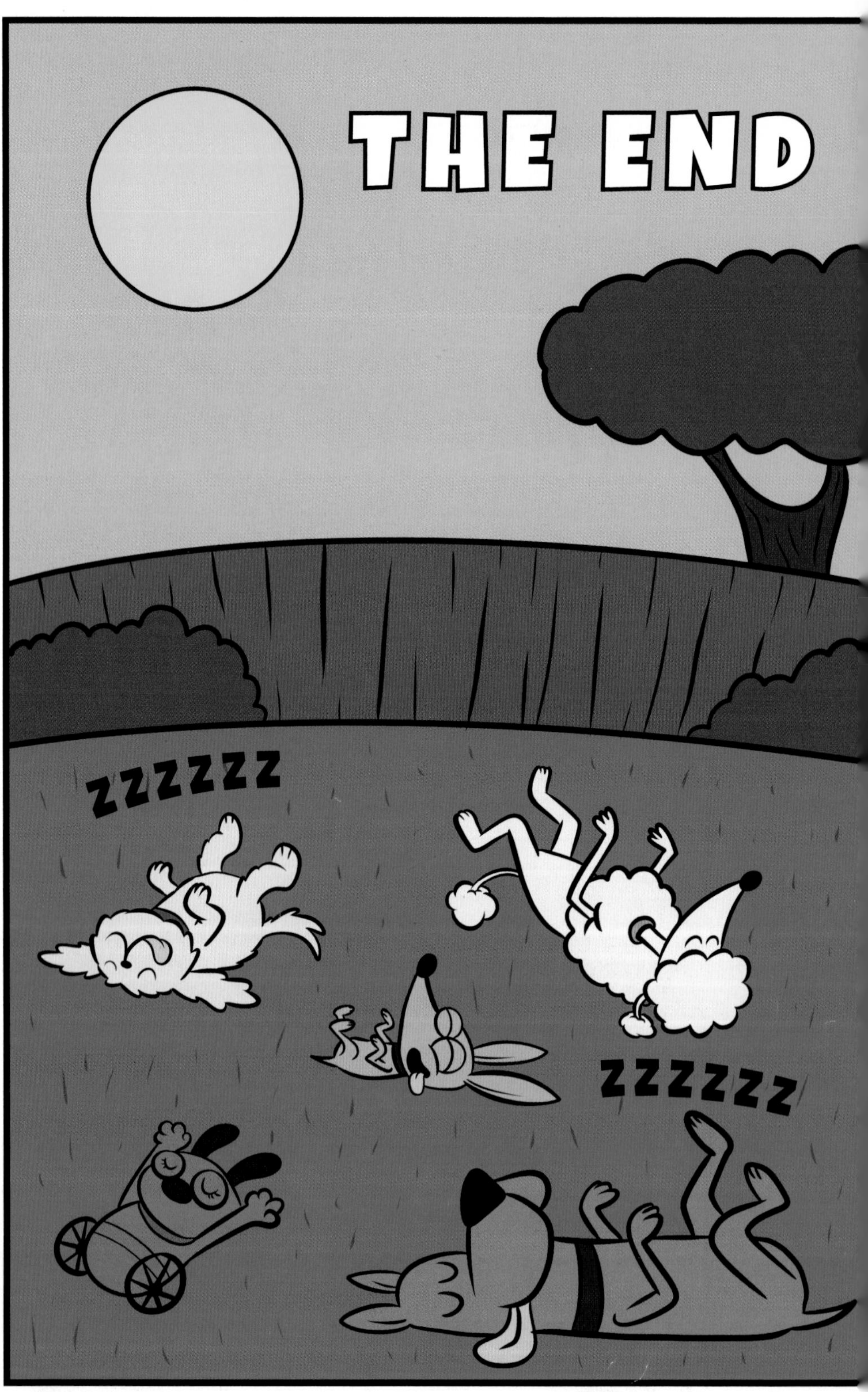
THE END
ZZZZZZ
ZZZZZZ